GEO

FLAWED LIGHT

Clare Curzon

severn
House

This title first published in Great Britain 2003 by
SEVERN HOUSE PUBLISHERS LTD of
9–15 High Street, Sutton, Surrey SM1 1DF.
Originally published 1972 as *Greenshards*
under the pseudonym *Marie Buchanan*.
This title first published in the USA 2003 by
SEVERN HOUSE PUBLISHERS INC of
595 Madison Avenue, New York, N.Y. 10022.

British Library Cataloguing in Publication Data

Curzon, Clare
    Flawed light
    1.   Detective and mystery stories
    I.   Title
    823.9'14 [F]

    ISBN 0-7278-5959-5

Printed and bound in Great Britain by
MPG Books Ltd., Bodmin, Cornwall.

CONTENTS

Part	Page
I: OLIVE	9
II: MEGAN	113

PART ONE
OLIVE

I

THE GLASS IS flawed. In the bottom lefthand pane is a small, irregular hole. If I put my finger there, into the tiny, flaked crater, I can feel a thin thread of wind blowing in. When I lean close, there is a minute, attenuated sound of stress.

Apart from that one small contact, the world outside is completely gone. Perhaps there is nothing out there in the dark. The window affords only a reflection of the lighted interior. A small, narrow room. A plaster wall. The tilted mirror; in it a face. The white face of a woman who looks up from writing, who writes in a small, narrow room.

So much that must be told, and I can only begin with this absurd hole in the glass! It means nothing to me. I don't even remember how it came there, or when. A stone flung up by the rotoscythe perhaps. I seem to recall some long-ago occasion when Edward was cutting the lawns. Was it this window then? It didn't happen at any significant moment, has no traumatic value that should make it so dominate me now. And yet it's as though it tries to prevent me writing down what I must explain. It won't let me.

No, the notion is absurd: *I* am preventing myself, trying with senseless chatter to cover the existence of something else, something fearful. Like a nervy hostess babbling to keep attention off a cobweb, or a lipstick

9

stain on a supposedly clean teacup, the cat urinating against the settee leg, a glimpse of her husband's hacked-off head she has overlooked after the murder...

And I am not to be put off in that way either. There is no call for fantasy. I will write of what is, simply that. And really I had already progressed beyond that stupid hole in the glass, to the window itself. A frame, a screen for the films that memory projects: Now Showing—a small, narrow room.

That is better. I do well to start there, for all my life is in this room. It's as though this room has always been. It's everything, *room-womb-tomb*.

Here it started, on that late April morning; and my life was broken open.

(No man is an island, he said; but then, I was not a man but a woman.)

Here I sat, complete in myself—someone sat here—and all was secure, quite enclosed. The little details of the lives around me no more disturbing than a murmur of distant traffic that increases the inner peace: a bare intimation of other existences mildly lapping at my shores.

And then Martine came in, flushed from the keen air outside, sparkling with sunshine, panting from her flight up the stairs. She threw open the door and stood there laughing.

"They've arrived. The new people at Greenshards. We just met them on the way back from the station. And, Aunt Olive, they're strange!"

I looked at her. Hair like corn-floss. A dead leaf lifted

by the wind had caught in the pompom of her mohair beret. I could faintly see last year's hemline on the camel coat I'd let down for her. Eleven years old. Radiant. The bearer of tidings.

When I look now at that picture the room has caught and eternalised there is one detail I cannot be sure of: the dead leaf on her beret. A dead leaf in Spring? That touch of mortality could be one my mind has added since. As I said, I'm not sure.

What I know is that then everything was changed. And I recognised it at that very instant. Strange people at Greenshards. New life.

Were we all in some way conscious that we would never be the same from then on?

Through lunch there was a new excitement in the air, busy speculation. Would they be selling off the paddock for a building plot? Were there children? And, if so...

"What are they like?" I asked.

They all stopped talking. The Neuchatel clock stalked stiff-legged behind us for a half-dozen ticks, while for them time was suspended. Then they looked at one another, questioning. They couldn't say.

I never was told how it came about that they met the Blanchards. Since then I have synthesised the scene myself.

They would have walked back over the wooden bridge singly, not in a group, and only Martine looking back towards the empty rails, craning to see if a train was signalled for the down line. Edward comes first to give up their platform tickets, turning away without noticing the collector, remote, almost reconciled, but for a further brief moment still deprived. Megan next, remembering to smile at the man, because of her public image and Edward's position and a dozen other surface reasons. But although she smiles, she holds her lips closely folded and her eyes are too bright, the colour high on her wide, Welsh cheekbones. They have gone in as four, and come out three.

Martine runs to catch them up, pulls at her father's arm and drives them into a group once more. "Couldn't we...?" She nods across to the Ice Cream Parlour.

There was no dead leaf on her beret then. Of that I am certain.

They would have humoured her. In some measure it helped to balance their offence: the other child sent away for his third term—the thrice-yearly ritual cutting of the cord.

We all shared in the guilt. Megan would wait until evening and then weep. Edward withdrew, murmuring platitudes. "It will be all right when he gets there. He'll soon shake down." For myself, I never went with them to the station. I said goodbye calmly, duster in hand, somewhere near the bottom of the stairs. When he had left I corded together the books and games from his room—'Scrabble', 'Monopoly', the table tennis things— and took them for their twelve-week exile in the linen-room cupboard. To the forgotten, narrow room under the roof, that looks out between chimneys to Green-shards through the trees. I sat down on the cane chair by the window and looked out. There was a small, splintered hole in the bottom, lefthand pane. Andrew travelled hourly farther away, accepting—but not yet understanding—expediency.

The Mintons met the Blanchards (like a game of Consequences) in the High Street. She said to him, "I hope you'll both be very happy here." He said to her, "We've been looking for somewhere peaceful. My wife has been unwell." The Consequences were—

That is the point: we don't know, can't yet tell for sure. So much. Perhaps—a life taken? Even now I cannot—

I went with Megan three days later to call on the new people at Greenshards. They seemed in no hurry to set the place to rights. Packing cases were still unopened on the chequered tiles of the unfurnished hall. They received us in the little study that looked out on the monkey-puzzle tree. I sat with my gloved hands in my lap while Megan and Giles Blanchard talked. Or rather, she babbled and he mainly waited for her to have done. His wife, Fenella, was there, silent and withdrawn, her huge apprehensive eyes fixing on us as though we were something alien and menacing. She was beautiful and much younger, it seemed, than her husband. Apart from murmuring a brief answer to one of Megan's queries she took no part in the exchanges, and respecting her preference for quiet, I let my eyes and mind rove over the walls I'd once known so well.

Someone had unpacked a tea-chest of books on to a mahogany desk, and I amused myself reading the titles from their spines and recalling passages I'd loved in just such copies on my father's shelves. I looked up to find

Mrs. Blanchard's eyes full upon me and a curious, wretched expression in them.

"I am afraid," she said, "I'm afraid I'm not a clever person like you, Miss Minton. hese are my husband's books. I find them mostly beyond me. I shall never be able to keep up with you."

Her voice trembled with some emotion close to despair. I had no idea how to answer her.

And that was almost all she said. The first words I was conscious of her speaking were significant, though. 'I am afraid.' Our visit did little to reconcile her to life in our small community.

Of Giles Blanchard what can I say, except that he did not surprise me? I had not pictured him, nothing like that—but had I done so, I'm sure he would have appeared to me much as he actually is, for he is somehow completely *right*, in every way. Throughout the whole of our strange relationship, it was to be the same: never was he in any manner surprising. It was as though he has always been known to me; as though, like this room, he exists outside time. But, just as I recognised that Fenella was apprehensive, so I remarked that he was immeasurably weary.

Giles, as I first saw him, at Greenshards. Giles Blanchard, later to be my husband.

They invited us, with Edward, for drinks in a week's time. "And you will see how well organised we shall be by then," Giles said, smiling. "Settling that date will spur us on with our unpacking. I promise, you'll be impressed."

Of course, we should have entertained them here first, but we understood that Mrs. Blanchard's nervous state made accepting invitations an ordeal at that time. I made some comment on this as we walked down the drive, saying how her neurasthenia must worry her husband.

Megan picked up the term and shook it about. Neurasthenia, why had I called it that? Since when had I qualified in medical diagnosis?

"But, Megan, it was Mr. Blanchard who said it was that. He told us she'd been in a nursing home for three months, you remember."

"He said nothing of the sort. He never mentioned her health. Really, Olive, sitting there day-dreaming like that. One day you'll upset somebody, putting words into their mouths. You would have done better to make some effort with his wife, poor colourless little thing. I don't think she opened her mouth to you at all."

I didn't argue. I remembered well enough what she had said, just as I knew her husband had called her neurasthenic. Megan is a dear creature, but like so many wordy women, she has lost, I think, the art of taking in. And, despite my earlier academic successes, despite too that I run her household with a smooth practicality she could never hope to achieve, she regards me as a little lacking—because, I think, I have never married. What would she have said then, I wonder, if I had told her all that was to happen? How I'd be back living at Greenshards one day, and married to the fascinating Giles Blanchard? Because he did fascinate her, that was evident. And I did by some uncanny means know, even as early as that, that he and I were destined for each other. The details of the pattern had yet to emerge, but already I could dimly make out the general shape. As it says, in a glass darkly.

The next week went by. Andrew's chair was removed from the dining-table and stood alongside the chiffonier. We became accustomed to his not being here. I sewed the last name-tapes on Martine's new summer uniform and she started back at the local day-school. It rained rather often and new buds kept appearing in the garden. I knew I should not be going with Edward and Megan to Greenshards.

There was no one point at which I made a decision. It was pre-ordained. I had no intention of presenting myself there in the face of such knowledge, and was prepared to plead a return of my sinus trouble for excuse. However, when the evening arrived, the woman who normally came to look after Martine sent a message that she had a bad cold, so I had no need of a fiction. Martine and I set out the Halma board in the lounge and began to play.

Even then Megan thought it necessary to try persuasion. She has never realised that although I am quiet I have ten times her determination. But Edward knows. He stood at the front door, tapping his gloves in one palm and apologising with his eyes. At length they left, formally using the front door and the drive, although for twenty-five years there has been a path directly between the two houses, by a gap in the beech hedge.

I allowed Martine to wait up for their return, for Edward is very correct about the duration of social visits, and it being Friday she would have no school next day. We played one game of Halma, and then I had a sudden fancy to hear some music. There being nothing suitable among the records by the radiogram, Martine opened the piano and stumbled through her Chopin Ballade. Despite her hesitations (or even because of them?) I found it strangely moving. Then we had a round of Snap and a second game of Halma.

It was during this last, while Martine thought out a move, that I experienced an overwhelming compulsion to stand up and go to the window. I went across, unlatched the french door and stepped out on the terrace. The child still bent over the table where we had been playing and seemed totally unaware that I had moved. I relatched the door quietly, and walking on the grass verge to muffle the sound of my steps, took the short way to Greenshards.

There was a low moon shining through the skeleton trees of the little thicket, and to reach the main door was caught up in the shadow of the old monkey-puzzle. As the dark image of the branches touched me I felt a shock of sharp spines as though I had been brushed by the tree itself.

The door stood ajar, and I pushed it farther open, remarking on the silence and darkness of the house. I did not know what I should find. Logically there should have been lights and voices, laughter in the drawing-room over on my right. But again, as when I first encountered Giles, there was a complete lack of surprise in coming upon him.

He was in the hall, slumped in a straight-backed chair

with curious carving on the deep wings that shaded his face. A crimson velvet cushion showed beyond one shoulder and now there were hangings of the same dark colour over towards the stairs. The beautiful chequered floor of black and white tiles was unspoilt by any carpet, but there were rugs of silky white fur here and there. A single chest of carved, dark wood stood in the square well of the stairway and Fenella's chair, to complement his own, at the far end: nothing beyond that. Giles looked calmly at me and said, without moving a muscle, "Thank you for coming."

I turned to my hostess. She sat asleep in her chair, with the straight, controlled bearing of some Ancient Egyptian statue. Perhaps the outline of her stiff, dark hair and the flat circle of enamel and gold about her neck, shining in the moonlight, increased for me this pharaohesque impression, but it was primarily the unusual disposition of her body that held my attention, that even made me momentarily afraid.

I murmured something, anything, to cover my abrupt appearance and brief stay, then turned and fled back the way I had come, not knowing how I should explain myself to Megan or the child.

As I reached the window, Martine picked up the Halma man. It was the one she had moved her hand towards as I rose to go. A wine-red soldier from the middle ranks right into the back of the new camp.

"There," she said proudly. "How's that?" With her no time seemed to have passed.

I sat down opposite her. "Very good," I said. "I'm afraid you're going to beat me this game."

She never had time to notice I was out of breath, for just then we heard her parents come in. They brought a sharp, outdoor atmosphere with them that I hadn't noticed on my furtive little expedition.

"They were sorry you couldn't come," said Megan. "Mrs. Blanchard seems to be quite taken with you." She sounded amused.

Edward took their coats and stood over by the opened piano. I had cleared away Martin's music but left the grand's lid back so that the warmth of the room might reach the inside. "Strange," he said, "but I could have sworn I heard you playing, Martine, while we were at Greenshards."

Megan kicked at a smouldering log on the hearth. She was wearing pretty, narrow shoes of black suede with a rhinestone pattern set in the high heels. (It is seeing such things that reminds me of my own condition, that I am almost a cripple. I drew back my right foot and tucked away in the folds of my housecoat the repulsive, black, surgical boot.)

Megan laughed again. "Probably what you heard was piped subliminal muzak. Just the sort of thing the Blanchards might go for. Really, Olive, you missed a treat. They've everything. No shortage of money there. Of course, it wouldn't appeal to all tastes, the way they've had the house done. Rather too severe on the whole. Dramatic, though."

"No," said Edward, still with his eyes on the piano. "It was Marty playing. I know where she goes a little wrong. I must have kept the sound in my mind, because I know you can hear nothing from one house to the other."

True enough. Not even a gunshot, in summer with all the windows wide and the gauzy white curtains floating like wraiths, those haunting veils that forever since have meant to me death and time's crude limits stamped over the eternity of childhood.

Edward realised immediately what he had said and looked quickly at me, so that I had to answer calmly, my hand reaching for a green soldier on the board. "Her practising does rather impress it on the memory. I think I hear it myself at times. Ballade in F Minor when I'm shopping at the supermarket." And I laughed.

"Yes, that was the piece I heard," he said.

Then, while we finished playing our game, Megan talked about Greenshards, as though it were some extension of her empire and leased to barbarians with the small advantage of wealth. She described the crystal glasses and the mirrors, the carpets and the antiques. She nearly went so far as to put a price on the lot. She spoke with some show of envy of Mrs. Blanchard's severity of dress and of the magnificent gold and enamel collar she wore. The entrance hall she didn't comment on. I knew without her telling us that she would have carpeted it wall to wall.

"I am sorry you were prevented from coming with us," said Edward, when Megan had gone upstairs with Martine. "I hope you don't mind strangers having taken Greenshards?"

Why should I mind? A house is a house and has a right to be lived in. Greenshards had been badly done by in that. Ever since Father's suicide there had been gaps in its ownership, changing sub-tenants, people merely flitting through. Now it seemed it was to have its full share of life again.

"No," I said, "I'm glad. I think their coming will make a difference to us all."

2

WE KEPT LOOSELY in touch with the Blanchards all summer, meeting them once or twice a fortnight, and yet I had the impression that by mid-June we were no closer to knowing them than on the day of our first brief visit. News of them came circuitously from the village. Strange, most people found them—just as Martine had said—and everyone had some fiction to pass on that illustrated his, or her, own interpretation of their strangeness. He drank, they said; she drugged; they had recently come into money after a partnership on the stage; they had mainly lived in South America; they had rubber estates in the Far East; both were foreigners naturalised British; he was a doctor, having sacrificed a career to devote himself entirely to a loved wife fated to die young.

We smiled each time a new story reached us and gave no more credence to one than to any other of the collection. In which we were wise enough, for all of them were slightly wrong. We stayed silent through all the speculation, for the Blanchards themselves had offered us no explanation of their origins, and Edward, being a local solicitor, was scrupulous in observing discretion. Despite what Megan calls my day-dreaming, I had no ready-made solution to their mystery, for I never did idly imagine them anyhow but where and as they then were. I had, moreover, the quiet conviction that there was no need to pry, for some day I should understand all completely, better perhaps than I knew myself.

For Midsummer's Eve we were invited to Greenshards for a small, late-night party. There were coloured fairy-lights strung along the terrace and the rosewalk, and as we sat sipping our drinks outside, we were aware of the pale foam of white roses suspended still and watchful in the dark, and beyond them a cumulus of trees that moved blackly as though disturbed by some silent and high-up wind that didn't reach us on the ground.

I found the night oppressive with memories. It was almost a physical hurt to have lost the past, and to be so far removed from the small girl who had once animated the quiet house behind me.

It was Megan who, with a sharp kick at my exposed ankle, drew my attention to the curious form the 'party' was assuming. As always before, we were the only guests, but now the two servants, a married couple called Fenwick, had abandoned their stations and were among us, glass in hand as we were. The woman had removed her white organdie apron and looked taller, even authoritative, in a dark dress that reached high at the neck and down to her wrists. On one shoulder she wore a large flat piece of metal jewellery I took to be Celtic, that had a dully shining stone at its centre. The man, in black tie and dinner jacket, was as unselfconscious as Edward or Giles.

"This is a special night," Giles told us, as though we had remarked aloud. "And I should like you, as our friends, to join with us in a little ceremony."

We returned to the house, which was in darkness. With

only a low table-lamp to guide us we made our way into the hall and stood behind the chairs Fenwick indicated. They were all identical with the two I had seen there before. We sat down. And almost immediately Mrs. Blanchard fell into a trance.

I find great difficulty in conveying what happened, for whereas some events are struck in black and white across my memory, clear as the instant image of a lightning-strike, others are confusedly obscured. I admit my mind was caught off guard. The depressing experience of nostalgia earlier on the terrace had stirred subconscious layers. It was not to function immediately with the scientific detachment I should prefer to bring to any suggestion of the occult. I cannot, for example, recall any of the conversation that followed Giles' invitation, apart from some ill-considered remark of Megan's, intended as a joke, about midsummer madness and spilling the blood of a white cockerel at the witching hour.

I did, however, attempt some assessment of the situation even as we sat there. With the inclusion of the Fenwicks in our circle, the rest of the house should be empty, and I recall now that Giles and Edward went through it to lock all outer doors and windows while we sat waiting. On their return Edward informed us, with a shade of embarrassment, that he had examined the mains electricity supply and that it was completely cut off. The table lamp that still dimly lit us from the hall's far corner had a battery for power and now Giles asked whether we should prefer it lit or put out.

"Oh, not total darkness!" Megan cried, as though she were as young as one of her own children. But I thought her fear genuine at the time and noted that there, in her Welsh, superstitious mind, any charlatan with skill might find a ready enough dupe. I hardened my own a little in compensation. Edward, I knew, would be meticulously fair, however much he regretted the occasion. There remained the Fenwicks, and their manner made me aware that they were quite used to this procedure. The smooth, almost professional way they took their places at the table prepared me to write them off as suspect: music-hall hypnotist and partner, or an 'ESP' team with a list of complicated clues all pre-learnt. As house servants they could, of course, have contrived to provide an alternative source of power for microphones and any levitation gear. In my heart I cried out against Giles for the unworthiness of the whole squalid little scene.

Fenella's head wobbled an instant, righted itself, then fell back against the crimson cushion, now dull and browned in the subdued light. She lay back limply, breathing deeply, eyes closed, and I marvelled how beautiful she was. Never had she seemed so lovely as then. And fragile. Perhaps it was in connection with that fragility that for an instant I thought of Spring and almost smelled the scent of hyacinths. Fenella began to babble of Cyprus.

It must have been shamefully evident to us all how eager she was to please, half-conscious as she was and half in what appeared to me, knowing nothing of these things, a sort of delirium. It was as though she flickered, passing in and out of some morbid state, so that I believed her part-genuine even as she began again consciously to strive for mental links with us. I supposed she was one of those nervous, inhibited creatures whose self-discipline sat heavily on an imaginative subconscious, and that now she tried to empty her repressed emotions through words associated with them. For it was certainly through words that she was reaching for some message. The word Cyprus recurred again and again in a mournful whisper punctuated by pauses and a little worried sequence of phrases about sunshine and sand, olive trees, lemons, goats, as she tried to catch up with the association. Then there was a change, a frightened struggle within her that lasted some seconds and had Giles rising from his chair. Mrs. Fenwick still held him by a hand, for we were all linked, and said the one word, 'Peace'. He subsided, and at the same instant Fenella gave a deep groan and fell slackly back in her chair. Her mouth was inelegantly open and the muscles of her neck, exposed in the feeble light, moved not at all.

There was a man's deep voice, muttering complaints. I distinguished the word 'foolishness' and then, dogmatically, 'Cypresses'. Like a radio announcer caught unawares by a switched-on microphone, he recovered himself and spoke evenly. We listened, petrified, although knowing it to be a trick, as he quoted some lines of poetry by D. H. Lawrence.

I forced my mind to run ahead to the end of the verse and then turned my head to look full at Fenwick. I must confess I don't know how it was done. I had not expected from his appearance that he could be so convincing an actor. Anyone who saw him would have sworn the voice had him completely at a loss. He was more than astonished: he was terrified. As I watched, my own flesh began to crawl.

Fenella's voice returned, wailing about some poor, broken white bird, all dead. And then, sadly, but in a normal tone, "Poor Giles, whatever will he do now?"

For a while there was silence but for her deep breathing. Megan rustled her dress across the table from me. I saw her release her hand from Giles' for an instant and pass it over her face as though she had walked into a cobweb. At the same moment I felt the same thing happen to me and shook my head ever so slightly. I thought I heard a child laugh somewhere out in the garden. But it was midnight almost, and all children would be in bed.

"Glass," said a small, breathless voice. "They're all smooth and sort of round. But broken. And so green but coloured like the rainbow!" The words came in a rush, high and excited, with rather prim diction. "Where did you find them? Show Livy!"

And the unaccountable occurred, for I felt the high, dark wind above the trees lift me and whirl me away. And then I was standing on my toes to reach my father's cupped hand and the ancient nacrine fragments of glass he had dug from the earth. He moved them with one finger so that I saw a dull gleam exposed where the sand fell away, and the surface that he rubbed clean was opalescent like green mother-of-pearl. If I look higher, I thought, I might see his face again. But I didn't dare, for fear of the terrible thing I should see instead. The great, bursting, bloody wound that was there in its place after he had shot himself. And being so afraid, I died.

They told me I had fainted, and considering my stupidity they were all very kind. But I saw Megan look at me with such speculation in her eyes that I knew she at least suspected me of wishing to attract attention. At once it made me abrupt and rude in my leave-taking, when in my heart I felt so very different.

I don't recall seeing Fenella again that night. I supposed Mrs. Fenwick had put her to bed. Giles came with us through the beech-hedge gap, but I wouldn't allow either Edward or him to support me. I felt older, almost middle-aged, and was exceedingly clumsy with my tiresome boot. I decided to avoid our neighbours for as long as possible and composed a cool little note of thanks for their hospitality.

Next morning—no, it was later the same morning, of course—Megan accused me of having produced the voice of the child at the end of the seance.

The days that followed were wretched ones, for Megan will never leave well alone, and her nervous energy compelled her to return again and again to the subject I wished fervently to forget. I could blame only myself for what had happened, for who among us could possibly have known of that scene when Father had come upon the ancient shards that suggested the name of our house? And then the pet name the child had called itself by was once mine. 'Livy', for Olive. No one there but Edward or myself had knowledge of that, nor of the fact that although precocious in many ways I had spoken of myself in the third person until I was seven or eight.

However willing I was to see the Fenwicks as villains

of the piece, I couldn't believe they had the means to find out such intimate items. And why bother with me? What gain could I possibly bring them? I had neither influence nor wealth. But perhaps I was mere expendable matter, the means of creating an impression on others who did count.

I longed to know what Giles had made of the occurrence, and how far Edward was implicated in this improper revelation of my past. But forever I returned to the question of my own responsibility in the phenomenon, for I admitted to having attended the seance in a mood of nostalgia and melancholy evoked by the house. Had I responded, too willingly, to some actual spirit-power that recreated a moment of the past? To think that was superstitious folly. It was more likely, as Megan had accused, that the eerie scene had over-stimulated my memory and I alone had caused the manifestation.

Certainly the others had heard the voice, as I had myself. But I had experienced much more. I had been moved, as though physically, to a different time and place. I had actually fingered the green fragments of mediaeval glass, touched a hand dead for twenty years, smelled the newly-dug earth and the sweet scent of hyacinths. Surely a hallucination, a symptom of hysteria. I was completely bewildered, at a loss to understand what were the facts. I knew only that I was deeply humiliated. Further, I was afraid that I might be mentally ill.

My intention to avoid Greenshards and our neighbours was made easier by two things at that time. Megan, after several months of idleness, was phoned by her

agent. She was wanted for audition for a television series.
The actress previously selected had had to withdraw and
the understudy was not quite suitable. It involved
Megan's travelling to London and staying overnight. She
returned next day delighted at having been chosen for
a principal part from a short list of three. Rehearsals
were to start almost at once and since the series involved
some outside filming, the location work was scheduled
to begin at the end of the next week. Meanwhile there
would be fittings for the wardrobe and sessions with the
make-up artists.

The house being empty therefore for the main part of
the day, I decided the time had come to start on the
redecoration of Andrew's room, ready for his return after
Summer Term. I set to at once, clearing the furniture
and stripping the main part of wallpaper the same day,
which was a Friday. One alcove I left over for the next
morning, because Martine would want to have a hand in
the work. She came shopping with me too, to choose the
new paper, and I had some difficulty dissuading her from
pictorial friezes which Andrew would certainly have out-
grown. There was a rather exciting one of galleons and
little ships tossing on inky strips of sea, but the whole
appeared too much turmoil for a room to sleep in. In the
end, with Andrew's love of mathematics in mind, we
chose a calm abstract of slightly irregular shapes set with
a series of fine spirograph patterns. The colours were
clear and the surface washable. I knew he would consider
it right.

After the weekend I intended to start on the woodwork, rubbing it down and applying the fresh white

gloss, but as soon as I began I was struck by such a piercing headache that I couldn't go on. Nor could I continue with any of my other work, for immediately I rose from lying down the terrible tension returned, affecting my sight so that even reading or letter-writing became out of the question. In despair at the chaos I had already caused in the house and seemed unlikely to be able to right by myself, I rang the local decorator who promised to send two of his men to finish the work for me. On arrival one of them went so far as to lecture me on taking on such a task. I understood him to mean he wouldn't trust me on a step-ladder. I assured him that I had in fact decorated all the upper rooms of the house regularly and defied him to fault the work. He acknowledged, on inspection, that it was quite properly done, but I then saw his real objection: that a hobby such as mine could menace his own, and his workmates', employment.

Well, I too have a job. It is to run Edward's home as comfortably and economically as I can. That I receive no wage for this duty is surely no reason for a worker who does to despise me as this man did? But it was not worth pursuing, for everyone assumes that as part of Edward's household I am comfortably off and so would have no right to take employment off a family breadwinner.

The man brushed off the dust from his sandpapering and opened his can of white paint. At the first breath of it I felt such violent nausea that I had to run from the room.

I came here, to the linen-room and sat, the day being

hot, by the open window. I made some effort to rally my senses and concentrate on what I had just been thinking, about the painter and my own status here. Logically there was no need for me to confine myself as I did to housekeeping. I had certain qualifications that would bring me enough to run a modest home of my own, and the annuity left me by Uncle Arthur had no strings attached. I was free to go. In that way I could be rid of the strong associations with Greenshards, keep independent of all who had witnessed that humiliating business at the seance.

By then I was feeling so wretched and unwell that I laid my head upon the sill and perhaps for a moment I slept.

Quite suddenly I was aware of being watched and quietly sat up. Across the slates, beyond a chimney stack, showed a small triangle of green, that marked the grass verge edging our drive. Standing disconsolately there and staring up at me was Giles Blanchard. At that distance, and with such pain as I then had in my eyes, I should not have been able to see his expression. Yet every line of his face was clear and his purpose was unmistakable. I knew then that I had horribly misjudged him and that he did not regard me as the eccentric exhibitionist I had appeared to myself. He did not recognise any need of mine for being excused ill manners and oddity. His own need, in fact, was all that preoccupied him then. And he seemed even more wretched than I.

I was halfway down the stairs to meet him when I felt the weight lift off my brain. I felt as free and light as my foot when the heavy surgical boot is removed.

He came dazedly into the hall and I drew him into the lounge where he stood blinking while his eyes became accustomed to the gloom. "My wife—," he said abruptly, "Fenella—begs you not to go. Please stay. I'm afraid she's going to die."

"What can I do? Shall I come across with you now?"

"There's no need. She'll be all right if I tell her..."

"I'm not going away. I hadn't even said I was going. I just thought I might, that is all."

"She was so very distressed. She told me to see you, beg you not to try running away. You can't escape yourself."

"But there's so much I don't understand, don't believe. That night, Midsummer's Eve, what happened? I'm afraid I behaved hysterically. I was too ashamed even to come and apologise. But if only she would explain to me...."

"I don't think she can. It happens through her, but afterwards she doesn't seem to know anything. Now she says she needs you to stay: she'll be finished if you go. Please, Miss Minton."

"I'm afraid. If I do stay, what will happen? What will become of us all?"

He looked at me strangely. "I thought perhaps *you* might know."

"No. Don't you?"

He shook his head.

Had he answered differently, had I been conscious of being over-ridden—compelled—in any way, I might have resisted the appeal. But it was clear he wanted me to choose. I believed then that I was to decide: I still do in some measure. What has happened since they came is that the seemingly impossible has become possible— but not inevitable. There is still this question of will. It all revolves on that.

"I will stay," I told him.

He turned away, relieved, then turned back. "Will you do one thing more? Will you stop fighting yourself? You're so severe. It's destroying Fenella."

I was suddenly filled with anger. The implication was monstrous, that what I felt, the self-criticism I tormented myself with, was in some way known and experienced by this other woman, little more than a stranger.

"No," he said hastily. "No, I see I've asked too much. But you must understand, she's not like other people. Or perhaps too much like other people. They seem to flow in and out of her mind. Not all the time, but when they're distressed particularly. And she has been very unwell these last two years. If I were to lose her, I don't know what I should do."

I knew. Standing there and seeing his agonised face I knew well enough. He would marry me. A demon part of me wondered whether Fenella had overheard that thought. "Tell her," I said briskly, "not to bother any more. I am not going away, and I am not going to make myself so busy that I cannot see her. I'll call tomorrow at half past ten, and if she's feeling well enough by then we'll have a little outing to the shops together. How will that be?"

"Wonderful," he said, pressing my hands. "Oh, you are good, so good!"

34

3

THERE IS A natural law that any creature acknowledged by its own kind to be different must be hunted down and driven out. That is how the species is kept strong and distinct. Man has the same underlying compulsion, however heavily disguised under social convention and cant. Where we fear, we protect ourselves aggressively. Such crises recur throughout history in pogrom and witch-hunt. We see it at present, overtly, in racism and rival with-it cults. It is built into each of us.

By which I don't seek to excuse myself, nor to admit that I consciously set out to get rid of Fenella. But already I *expected* her to die, from remarks Giles sometimes made, and also because I interpreted as for her the reference to death that occurred at the seance. Giles too, I was well aware, had recognised those lines from *'Giorno dei Morti'*; and in what other context could he see them, when taken together with the words that had followed in Fenella's normal voice? 'Poor Giles, whatever will he do now?'

And so, expecting her to die, I came to accept it. From acceptance it is not a long step to hope. I did not see this at the time, but now in retrospect I recognise this darkening recess in my mind. To wish for the destruction of another being, a human life brought to nothing—but a curiously empty life, almost a nothing even while there is breath: is that so terrible? To negative a negative is surely a means of creation.

Whatever the understanding I might later arrive at, at that moment I admitted to only a sense of alarm and revulsion.

I kept my word to Giles. I neither left the village nor kept myself so occupied that I had no time to see his wife. I saw her constantly, watched her, with brisk bonhomie gleaming in one eye and calculation in the other. I evolved a technique of skating swiftly over a series of surface matters that left her unpractical mind bewildered with details. It was an uncharitable enough ploy, on a level with confusing a child with polysyllables, but it enabled me to secure some privacy from her strange telepathic habits. (I almost wrote 'power', but I was soon to find it was not that at all, for power implies some action. She was not exerting any influence at all. It was more in the nature of a mental implosion that occurred; nature's abhorrence of a vacuum.)

Chatter does not normally come easily to me and I tend, rightly I think, to despise it in others. Now I pursued it with as much apparent verve as Megan herself in the throes of one of her more corgi-like enthusiasms, fussing her way into trivia. But even then I needed to be wary, for part of me would stand back and mock the conversing one, and Fenella, weary with the effort to follow my thread, would glaze over and somehow have access to that other silent half of me. It was uncanny how close she sometimes came to plumbing how I really regarded her.

I saw that it was quite safe to question her about her

dabblings in the occult, for as long as I kept the matter on the level of intelligent enquiry she appeared out of her depth. As Giles had said, she really did not appear to know what happened, let alone how. She had not enough brain to organise a deliberate hoax, which meant that either Giles or the Fenwicks, or all three in collaboration, had arranged the 'emanations' that had so upset me at the end of the seance. While admitting that my attitude had been more conducive then to hallucination than normally, because of the depressive associations of the house, I couldn't dismiss the whole experience as imaginary, for all the others had heard what I heard. The fraud was therefore a vocal one, and any experience I had, beyond what the others sensed, might have been due to my having received some hallucinogen drug. The Fenwicks had served our meal between them, and Giles had carried my coffee across the terrace when we re-arranged the chairs. Any of them had the opportunity of doctoring what I ate or drank. But who of them could have acquired the uncommon information of my father's find a quarter-century before? And have known that it was spring, with hyacinths in bloom? The only person outside myself was surely Edward. And Edward alone would recall the forgotten pet-name 'Livy'. Knowing his formality, I could hardly believe he would offer such intimate trifles in conversation with a new acquaintance. We are a withdrawn family and not given to sharing confidences.

"He goes to the 'White Lion' most evenings," said Fenella suddenly one afternoon when an unaccustomed silence had fallen between us. "I believe he plays darts there. Or is it dominoes?"

"Who does?" I demanded in amazement.

"Fenwick. You asked me what he did to amuse himself."

Did I? I wasn't aware of having spoken, but certainly that question would have followed logically enough on how I'd been probing. But that was equally true of what I'd been thinking privately. In some way both strains had met at that one point. I walked on as though unconcerned. "So he meets quite a lot of people from the village?"

"I suppose so. He does mention them from time to time."

I turned in my mind the possibility of asking Edward to call in at the 'White Lion' some night and see who these villagers were, for they might well be the source of information a medium could use and attribute to supernatural knowledge. But I preferred not to voice my uneasiness to Edward. I steered the conversation into channels that were less personal and became determined to keep greater guard over my subconscious thoughts.

Under normal conditions it appeared that Fenella didn't absorb my experiences from a distance. (It is not that she couldn't, but that other matter had access to her more easily, or she to it.) The fact that she had seemed to do so when I was considering throwing all up and leaving Edward's home, could have been due to the intensity of my feeling at that time. So much I can accept, that telepathy may exist when emotion is so overpowering. But usually she required to be near me, and increasingly I came to see that the leakages, as I called them, were more due to my occasional lack of vigilance than to her prying. Not that she made no efforts to penetrate my mind, for I was conscious of it in some non-physical manner that was equivalent to being touched by the fingers of a blind person. She even asked apologetically if I would consent to sit again with the same circle while she exercised her 'gift'. Always I made some excuse, and once before Giles. I observed he smiled at this, as though it were only what he would have expected. And I was conscious that he approved of my decision.

Over a matter of weeks I believed I was getting the measure of my opponent. For that is what I knew her to be. And perhaps I became over-confident, for one day, foolishly, I put my palm in her hands as we sat in the garden at Greenshards, and challenged, "There now, let's see if you can read my fortune."

She didn't peer into it as I had expected, but squeezed it softly and looked away from us. For a moment she said nothing, then gave a little startled cry like a child surprised. "Why do you call yourself 'Miss'?" she asked innocently.

"Why not?" I demanded. "I am a woman, and I've never married." It was such a silly thing for her to have said, but her idiocy went further. "Are you *sure*?" she insisted.

Giles called her to order, but I wasn't offended. Nor was she. "Well, you will be then," she said. "He's a relative, a cousin. And there is another. You marry twice."

Mortified, I pulled my hand away and rose to leave. She had no need to fabricate such fairground romances for me. I was not to be entranced with the promise of a tall dark stranger. But then, I remembered, it wasn't a stranger she had foretold. A relative, a cousin. I had no more than one cousin and he would have taken me only from pity. In any case, he wasn't free.

There were quick steps after me as I hobbled home. Giles caught me up easily. "That was unfortunate," he sympathised. "She will say anything, the first thing that comes into her head."

He didn't attempt to claim it was a possible prediction. We walked side by side a moment and then I dared to speak what I felt. To anyone else it would have been improper, but it seemed that Giles already understood enough.

"It must be difficult," I said, "for anyone so beautiful as Fenella to imagine, for a moment, what it is like to be —as I am."

His reply was oblique. "My mother was Spanish," he said, "so that is my second tongue. We have two verbs, 'to be'. The distinction is a physical one, but there is a metaphysical equivalent in my mind. With Fenella it is 'estar', but for you always 'ser'. I find both of you beautiful, with the same distinction between. Your beauty is a permanence, part of your essence. Fenella happens to be lovely now, in the same sense that she happens to be in the house or in the garden. Do you understand?"

Not really. But it was an interesting enough point to interrupt my self-pity, which in any case I've had long practice at curbing. It was thoughtful of him. He is more clever than one would suppose.

Next day Andrew returned from school for the Summer Holidays. He was changing, and knew it, but he thought the process already complete. Lounging against the cold radiator in his window recess, he was nevertheless very much on his own feet. He looked coolly about him at the familiar room of his childhood. "You've done it up," he said. "Nice wallpaper."

His preoccupation of the moment was the impact on the family of his new, detached self. Soon the superior smile would come, the mocking: 'Oh, Aunt, this is the seventies,' or even 'but we're in the twentieth century now'. When ultimately exasperated he would be calling back over one shoulder the added taunt, 'A.D.!' I had known this had to come, but not that it would begin so soon.

So keen to fault us all, and me in particular since we'd once been close, he would pick upon the least, thoughtless word let drop at table and subject it to silent analysis, smiling while his knife and fork dissected with finicky niceness some once-favourite dish I'd planned would break through his sophisticated superiority. And then, later, gleaming with an acquired malice, he would use the new information he had picked up. It wasn't long, therefore, with Megan's flow of unconsidered chatter increased by the whirl of outside activity she now revolved in, that he overheard some reference to that wretched occasion of the seance. It delighted him, and from then on when we were alone there was an endless tapping under tables and falling of pictures from walls, and once a puff of unaccountable whitish vapour that rose behind his chair as we sat reading, he with his hands innocently open to my eyes.

"You go," I commented, "to great lengths to make your point, which is not, perhaps, a very well informed one." The jokes ceased then, but I had lost, for the further he progressed to being a man the further I receded into my tortoiseshell quaintness, over-precise and unapproachably spinster. My one defence, my cultivated ugliness. Soon I would be totally unacceptable. Andrew would be lost to me.

He sensed something of my distress and briefly tried to compensate.

"You know my cricket bat you oiled? Best colour of the lot. Venables says it's the best in Junior School."

Venables the new godling. I knew I should grow to detest his name by the holiday's end.

When Andrew had been with us for a week, Martine's school broke up. She seemed overtired and listless, but recovered enough to enjoy a shopping expedition to equip her for her week of pony-trekking. I hoped that the fresh air and exercise, together with the change of disciplines, would restore her energy. She barely saw her mother in the few days she was at home before leaving, for Megan had daily rehearsals in town and spent only two nights a week with us. I had the impression that there were interests beyond the acting that kept her so much from home.

On the Thursday before Martine was to set out, Megan rang from the station that she had caught an early train back. Edward was busy with some papers in the study and I took out the car myself to go and fetch her. She was waiting in the road outside, in the little oblong marked TAXIS which so seldom holds any vehicle at all. She looked sleek and city-bred and although she kept conversation to the normal trivia of family enquiries I sensed in her a tremendous inner excitement that she could barely contain.

She waited, however, until after dinner when I brought coffee for her and myself into the study with Edward's. Martine had been sent to bed, with the excuse of her early departure next day, though I thought she would have slept better for a little time spent with her mother first. Andrew had gone about some private business of his own.

"Now," said Megan with relish, "I have something to tell you which I'm sure you'll find interesting. It's about the Blanchards."

It appeared that she had met, through a friend of a friend connected with the producer, a naval officer who had known them nearly twenty years before.

She paused to appreciate the effect of her news. Edward and I sipped coffee and looked unimpressed.

"But, don't you *see?*" said Megan impatiently. "*Twenty* years ago. Mr. and Mrs. Giles Blanchard. Now how old do you take Fenella to be?"

I saw her point. So apparently did Edward. "There's nothing to prevent the man from marrying more than once," he pointed out.

"But how often," scored Megan, "to a woman called Fenella? I mean, is it likely? They were married in Plymouth twenty years ago last May. Do you know what

43

I think? That woman's no more Fenella Blanchard than I am. What's more I'm going to prove it!"

The appalling thing was that she meant it. She had actually invited this Lieutenant-Commander for the coming weekend, with the specific intention of arranging a confrontation. Edward was as horrified as I was. He tried to reason with her: he insisted that, even if she were right in her suspicions, there was no cause for her to intervene in so private a matter. But Megan's probings had disturbed a swarm of bees that now buzzed ominously in her bonnet. There was no satisfying her. She was out to precipitate a scandal, whatever the cost, and Edward for once squarely accused her of this. "Any scandal," she said self-righteously, "will not be of my making but theirs. Heaven only knows what state of affairs they are trying to cover up. If this one calls herself Fenella, where in heaven's name is the real one? What have they done with her? And why? According to Sammy" (the naval officer forsooth!) "she was a very wealthy woman."

"So," retorted Edward, "is this one, and I couldn't possibly afford a slander suit brought by her. When will you learn that there are legal ways of verifying whether the situation is as irregular as you seem to suspect?"

"Much good will they do," she said with scorn. "What would you find? A record of the marriage, with the date I quoted, and a description of a Fenella that doesn't fit this one at all. And how would they account for that? By claiming that she's older than she looks, has had a face-lift or some monkey-business with her glands? Because the real one should be middle-aged and grey by now. And there's another thing—no, don't get up Olive; I'm determined you shall hear this because it sounds pretty ominous to me. You ought to hear what a possible monster we have living amongst us—do you know *why* they left Plymouth some ten years back? Because their home was burnt down. There was talk of some wild party there, and afterwards, during the night, the whole place went up in flames. Not everybody got out. One person was burnt to death. At the inquest she was identified by Blanchard as the young *au pair* girl, but he'd little enough to go on. The body was accepted as hers because everyone else was accounted for."

Megan leaned forward and drew every drop of theatre out of her next words. "*Mrs Blanchard*—or so he said— Mrs. Blanchard was unable to attend the inquest because she was in a nursing home some thirty miles away, suffering from exhaustion and shock. The coroner expressed his sympathy. Since then the Blanchards have never reappeared in the locality—"

"Megan, this is utter madness." Edward's coffee cup rattled as he thrust himself out of his chair. He strode across to the cabinet and poured a glass of Scotch.

"It is." Megan nodded, with satisfaction. "But not mine. His. His and hers. You've always agreed with me that there's something very strange..."

There was no shaking her. She had worked it out and decided it must be so.

"I utterly forbid you," said Edward through clenched teeth, "to have that man to the house."

"Giles?" asked Megan, mocking him.

45

"The other one. Have you told him what you suspect? How far have you spread this preposterous story?"

I left them there and let myself out on to the terrace. They might have heard me telephoning from the hall, so I had to go myself through the beech-hedge into Greenshards' garden.

I have no idea where Fenella was, but I found Giles in the conservatory, spraying some fuchsias. Abruptly I asked him not to question what I said, but to refuse any invitation Megan might spring on him for the weekend. She was planning something unsuitable, I said. It would serve only to upset Fenella.

He stared at me as though from a great distance, then put down the insecticide gun on the trestle. "Of course, Olive," he said quietly. "I'll take care to do as you say. You know I have complete confidence in your discretion."

I almost ran back to Edward's study, and let myself silently in. They were still in dispute and seemed not to have noticed my movements. But by now I could see that Megan would be having her way.

In the event, the Lieutenant-Commander's visit was a fiasco, for the man was something of a bore. And when Megan rang Greenshards to issue her invitation there was no reply. Later we heard that Giles and Fenella had just left for a long weekend in Kent.

So we entertained Megan's 'friend-of-a-friend-of-the-producer's' and I observed that although she was vexed at the non-appearance of the 'guilty pair' they were to expose, yet Megan managed to extract a deal of gaiety from the visit. For myself, I was relieved when on Sunday night we all accompanied her Sammy to the station and saw him off on a train for London.

Next morning, to break the silence of the breakfast table, I remarked that this was the day the Fenwicks were due to fly off to Malta on holiday.

Megan arched her elegant eyebrows. "Well, that shows they're not superstitious."

Edward, buttering his toast, looked up. "Why superstitious?"

"The seance, of course. Have you forgotten all about the cypresses, and priests burying someone? And then that spooky touch about the 'broken white bird, all dead'? Well, you'd think that if they really believed in clairvoyance they'd be a little more cautious. I shouldn't care to fly to the Med myself right now. But there are none so unimpressed by stage effects as those who rig them."

"Do you think it was a fake, Aunt Olive?" asked Andrew jauntily.

Edward interrupted by clucking over the time and making a more fussy departure than was customary, but I don't believe in evading children's questions. I started to stack the plates, and when Andrew passed his, our eyes met for an instant. "I don't know," I said.

"Well, what would you prefer the explanation to be?"

The trouble was that I didn't know even that. I hadn't dared to examine myself frankly.

"I should prefer," I told him, "it never to have happened at all."

"But it did," he insisted.

"Yes. It did."

I was saved further probing, for the boy left later that day for a fortnight under canvas with friends from his old prep school. Megan returned to her theatrical round and by Tuesday the house was silent and deserted again. I put things to rights and came up to the linen-room to get on with the mending.

Instead I found myself sitting at the window, staring out. The view seemed strangely unfamiliar: the whole layout of roof, chimneys, trees and garden appeared to have shifted slightly to a new perspective. The spatial relationships were wrong, as though more than one scale of size obtained. I had the disquieting sense that years had gone by since last I sat there.

I noticed then that there was a small, almost round hole in the lower lefthand pane, as though some pebble had been catapulted through. I put my finger into the tiny, flaked crater and felt a cool, thin thread of wind blowing in. I leaned close and heard the minute, attenuated sounds of stress. No louder than sea-noises in a conch, but somehow terrible.

4

I HAVE LOST half a day.

When I came up here it was almost noon. Now it is quite black outside and someone must have turned on the light. Strangely I am not hungry, but tired and smoothed out all at once. And somehow light-headed. My right arm is stiff and the fingers cramped.

It is a little alarming. I have been down to look around the house and everything appears to be in order, but nothing gone from the foodstuffs since breakfast. The tray I had prepared for my lunch is still there untouched. Yet I feel I have eaten. Is it possible that I went out for a meal and have forgotten since my return? Perhaps there is someone who saw me? Should I go across to see Giles? He might know what has happened. But what could I ask him?—'Did you chance to notice me wandering about, because I lost myself for a few hours? Oneself is such a tiresome thing to lose.'

It is all right. I was there, at Greenshards. Giles says not to worry, everything is under control. He told me to write it all down, whatever happens. He says he told me this once before and that is what I have been doing. But the pages have all been tidied away somewhere. I have to find them and put them in order, number them. He says I must relax. If I do that everything will be much easier for us both. He speaks of 'us' and 'we'. Fenella was asleep again, like an Egyptian princess, so we were able to talk without her hearing. Giles is very tired. I think he is under a great strain.

He says Edward will be coming home shortly and I must relax. Then I shall seem like I was before. Edward mustn't suspect. I shall go on doing everything exactly as was my custom. I am the same person. There is no conflict in me. I shall trust Giles completely and it will be all right.

It is only strange this time, he says, because I have been gone for so long. The other times I was away only for a fraction of a minute. This time it was for hours, *and now I know*. This time I went in the flesh: more of me is moving as one. I guessed this when I found mud on my heels, and a crumpled beech leaf clinging to my skirt.

I even remember now where I put the manuscript away. I have to sort it and number the pages. Then I will add these two to them. It is an important document: the account, phase by phase, of a unique experiment.

It has to succeed: there is so much at stake.

This morning, by first post, came a picture postcard from the Fenwicks. They have arrived safely after a pleasant flight, and the hotel is quite comfortable.

So—no disaster, and the prediction of death has yet to be fulfilled. Megan may be wrong in thinking it referred to them, in which case...but there is still the flight home. Accidents do often happen at take-off. If so, and the Fenwicks die, then Fenella will have had her reprieve.

She will live on. They must come back safely. I cannot bear to wait for their return.

Giles has lent me some books about psychic phenomena. Sometimes I believe, but at others my reason revolts. Telepathy, yes: so many people have experienced this, privately. I have done so myself, without ever admitting. He says the conscious mind exercises a jealous censorship over the subconscious, and so its experiences become like something too shameful to admit to. He says that to be a full person one must understand these restrictions and learn to evade them. Then we may enjoy what blunter mentalities call extra-sensory experience, but which is truly normal—not morbid at all—if one's mind is fully capable. In time, he says, he will prove this to me. I think perhaps he will.

But precognition, foretelling the future, that I know is against the nature of things, for every event must have a cause that precedes it. No event can have an effect before it has happened. Knowledge too cannot exist apart from a brain; and how could we assume, in accepting precognition, that some mind in time-to-come transmits this knowledge to us?

Why not? he says. What is time? With all our vaunted science we can as yet measure it only in three-dimensional space. Can we measure the extent of a mind?

I spoke to him of will-power, but he doesn't like the word. He talks instead of energy from the very core of one's existence: it is the source of all instinctive behaviour. Other energies we create are lesser ones, the result of friction and reactions within the mind's layers.

We must channel the central energy through all layers of existence, conscious or otherwise.

But I continue to function in terms of will, and it is really the same thing that he speaks of. There are parts of me he does not know about; how much will it has taken to become me, and to survive. This is what makes me stronger than others. I wonder if he thinks he is stronger than me? I shall not tell him about what I discovered as a child, but I shall write it down now, because this is an important document, an account of a unique experiment, just as he says.

There was a period at which I used to dream a lot. Looking back, it seemed at first to me that I must have been thirteen or so, because of the maturity of my thoughts, but, on observing the children here, Edward's children, I have found there is an age at which these dreams particularly trouble them, and it is quite a while earlier, from eight or nine on. With me these were dreams of actuality which accelerated into unbearable suspense. There was a hint of pursuit that recalled the bear-chases of early childhood nightmares, but above all was this towering sense of doom closing inevitably in. I used to fear sleep, fight against being overtaken by the inescapable reality of the dream. And then, once, suddenly I recognised—whether asleep or awake I can't remember —that the dream was my own, that *I was making it*. It seemed to me that since this was so, I could make it good or bad. And I determined that when this happened again I would stop in my tracks and remake it even as it happened.

This I did. Asleep as I was, when the dream began and

the nightmare grew from it, I remembered my resolution. I said inside myself, 'This is *my* dream. I can make it as nice as I want.'

I don't remember whether there was a good dream next, but there certainly was no bad one. This happened for several nights in succession. After that I was never troubled by nightmares. I knew too that something very important had happened to me.

I don't know what Giles would make of that, since he doesn't care to use the word 'will-power'. But I do. I believe I can consciously direct myself away from the harmful, a firewalker who doesn't experience pain and whose feet remain uncharred from contact with the glowing embers. I am in control. He doesn't suspect to what extent this is so.

Megan's friend is to visit us again. She is determined to stage this confrontation, whatever Edward says. It is quite clear what I must do, and it should not be difficult.

Tonight Megan presented her melodrama. It was a complete failure! And how much better this way, with no one disturbed by any unpleasantness and the poor Lieutenant-Commander quite oblivious of the crosscurrents he has been piloted through. Only Megan was disconcerted, and that momentarily, for the fiasco so infuriated her beneath the social surface that her eyes flashed and her voice shrilled, making her appear even more delicious to the besotted man. Since he is foolish enough to be unable to mask his admiration, she was finally appeased and the evening ended with her lavishing affection on all her guests, almost indiscriminately.

Edward, at first ashamed for her and stiffly on his dignity, thawed and relaxed. He believes that all is well now with his charming little wife. For her he is even prepared to like the new acquaintance and overlook his fatuity. He hasn't guessed yet that they are lovers.

It was her vanity that played into my hands, for she spent so long dressing for dinner that her Sammy was left unattended. (Edward was lingering in the study on the pretext of studying some papers for an injunction application next day.) It was perfectly normal for me to suggest that the guest would enjoy a stroll in the garden while the others finished dressing.

We skirted the house (admired the bizarre front elevation and the pretentious additions Uncle Arthur had seen fit to attach in an attempt to match the elegance of Greenshards) and passed, without his observing that any frontiers were crossed, through the opening in the beech hedge. We moved slowly, for my leg was troublesome, past the little spinney of birches, towards the river. And there, in the shadows of the boathouse, we saw the tiny glow of red light where Giles awaited us, drawing on his cigar.

It took the Lieutenant-Commander some seconds to adjust his sight after the clear summer evening outside, and when he was able to make out the figure facing him, Giles nodded, his eyes not leaving the other man's. I knew I had done all that was required of me and I left them together. Halfway back towards the spinney I looked behind me. All I could make out of them was the red tip of Giles' cigar moving back and forth, rhythmically as though it swung suspended from a string. Sammy came back alone, some fifteen minutes behind me.

Later, when the Blanchards arrived, they were introduced and, for all his foolishness, not the flicker of a single facial muscle revealed that Sammy had come upon Giles earlier that evening. His manners were perfect as he turned to Fenella (coaxed for once to appear outside her own domain) and he was convincingly sincere when he swore he would have known her anywhere, for she hadn't changed by so much as a hair from their last meeting some eighteen years before. Nor for that matter, he said—turning gravely back to her husband—had Giles; although I, who watch so closely, have seen him age even in the few months he has lived beside us.

Megan was frustrated, but flattered back into a sweet temper by the sailor's attentions; Edward relaxed, Giles gleamed with satisfaction and looked intently at me with a secret smile as if to say, 'You see? What can they do to me? I am more than a match for any of you.' But the surprise of the evening was Fenella.

Normally so vapid and languorous, tonight she scintillated. On reflection I see it was less what she actually said than her manner which was vivid. It was as though a beautiful waxwork came alive. Yet for all that, Giles took her home early, fearful that she might become overtired. But it was he, not Fenella, who, as the dinner party went its way, grew strained and stumbled over his words. He had a little nervous tic that fluttered a muscle at the corner of one eye. Edward observed this too and understood that it was due to fatigue, for as host he was able to appreciate how little alcohol Giles drank. When they had gone he reproved Megan gently for the remark that their neighbour was 'well under'. Edward is never slow at appreciating the negative virtues; it is flamboyance that too easily deceives him.

But the evening had not run out of marvels even then. As I moved about the lounge, removing ashtrays, shaking cushions and examining polished surfaces for any trace of moisture from spilt glasses, the telephone rang. Fenella had discovered her little sequinned bag was not with her. It would be, she thought, still in the dining-room by the table leg where she had sat.

I looked into the eye of the mouthpiece, and the telephone was transfigured into a most beautiful and rare thing, for the voice that spoke belonged to neither of the Blanchards. I steadied my own voice to reply. I asked the caller to be so good as to wait while I checked. The bag was where Fenella thought she had left it and I brought it back with me, confirmed that all was well and added, "It's good to know you are back, Mrs. Fenwick. Did you have a good journey?"

"It was lovely," she said. They had returned yesterday by the night flight and nothing had ever been so beautiful as passing over the lighted cities of Europe. It was like looking down at the stars instead of up.

I knew how it felt, for I stood then looking out on the terrace and the whole night swooned with stars so that they wheeled all about me and nothing was real or important except the fact that the Fenwicks had returned. No aircrash, no cypresses, no red-robed choristers, no requiem on some Mediterranean hillside. The prophecy was not yet fulfilled, the death it spoke of was for someone else. The dead white bird, all broken, had another meaning.

I thought of Giles leaning over that second carved chair in his hall, calling on his wife to wake up. 'Fenella; dove, open your eyes.' I saw her eyes closed for ever.

In my heart I thanked Giles for the ulterior message of the phone call, spoke my thanks to his housekeeper and quietly replaced the receiver.

"Was that for me?" Megan called down from the landing. "What is it, Olive?"

"Nothing important," I told her. "Mrs. Blanchard left her bag, that is all." I turned off the downstairs lights and when I reached the landing Megan was still there, looking curiously at me.

"Oh, by the way," I added, "the Fenwicks are back. They took the night flight yesterday."

"Well, so much for predictions," said Megan, shrugging and running a hand through her red curls.

"Is it? We shall see," I promised.

Next day the Lieutenant-Commander departed for London and Megan stayed on for another night. Two hours after she left on Monday Martine arrived back from her pony-trekking. Andrew still has another week away.

It happened so suddenly. If there were indications to warn us, they were only slight, having no significance until it was too late. Had we understood them, still it would have been utterly useless. It was inevitable, old Hepworth said. Sooner or later it had to be. A small blood vessel in the brain: merely a matter of time to its rupture.

We were in the garden, but not together. She had put down the jug from refilling her birdbath and knelt to shake out a mixture of crumbs and ham scraps round its plinth. I was aware of her vaguely as part of the garden that had moved and then stopped moving. I looked more closely, putting down my mending, a frayed collar on a cricket shirt of Andrew's. She went on kneeling there without movement. I left my deckchair and called to her, "What is it? Get up, dear."

She half-laughed. "I—can't."

I saw her make an effort, sway and fall slowly forward on to the pillar which rocked twice and toppled. It took me an eternity to reach her.

She seemed asleep, but breathing strangely and I was afraid to touch her. Mrs. Benson, swabbing the kitchen floor, came when I called, and then I fled to the phone. Dr. Hepworth was out but his partner came and took her himself to the cottage hospial.

She lived on another nine hours, gently and invisibly bleeding, but never woke again. We waited in corridors or briefly about her bed, and just after two o'clock, as the world outside was being renewed, she left us.

Martine, little doll, those few years of memories, that fragile link with a future beyond our own, finished.

I had known when they took her up, and the thin arm swung, showing where sunburn and paler skin pathetically met at the edge of her aertex blouse. Looking down, I saw the last of the water spilled, the red plastic jug on its side, long spout pointing to the shattered birdbath: the little white, stone sparrow that had sat on its edge, broken.

Requiescat in pace, Martine Isobel Minton, aged eleven, beloved daughter...

Hair like corn-floss. Martine, radiant, sparkling with sunshine, standing forever in my doorway, a dead leaf caught in the pompom of her mohair beret. *Martine.*

5

NOTHING WILL EVER be the same. And yet all continuing so true to form, changing only in intensity. The
summer hotter, the sky more treacherously blue, the
roses fuller. Edward more remote and ashamed, Megan
more explosive, Andrew travelling farther from us all.
And I? Anaesthetised perhaps.

They didn't tell the boy. She said it wasn't fair to him,
away on holiday. But the truth was they didn't know
how. Edward, apprehensive that she would smother the
child with fierce possessiveness, agreed to leave it till
Andrew came home. It gave her time to start fighting
back. And with what wild fury she at first fought, accus-
ing anyone who might in any way be imagined responsible for her hurt. Me, for being there, Hepworth for
not, faceless other children who at some time might have
played too roughly. She wanted Martine's pony shot.

Nothing could persuade her that a tiny, unsuspected,
perhaps inborn weakness could alone have so monstrous
an effect. Someone must be to blame. Someone had to
suffer for it.

Andrew returned to the fact of his sister's death, dis-
section and burial, and the total conception was too
immense for him to deal with. He thought it—or accused
it of being—a macabre joke, and the tortured smile he
seemed always to wear on approaching his parents re-
pelled them, even when they most needed to hold him

and reassure themselves with the touch and the sound
and the smell of his vitality.

Briefly he turned to me in his efforts to grapple with
what he couldn't reach. And I accepted him back,
although knowing that it signalled the beginning of our
complete severance.

He asked me and asked me again. And I told him,
passionlessly, factually, as earlier I had said over with
him his eight-times table that he used to get wrong, his
Latin declensions, Boyle's Law. I made it relate for him
to all these other wordy things and then he was free to
go away and begin to understand. In time it overtook
him and then there were two days of defeat and terror
when he clung, shaken with ugly, grating cries or leaning, beaten and defenceless, against my shoulder as I
pretended to continue with some household unnecessity.
He bared himself so completely that I knew he would
never forgive me once he had grown some defence.

Passively and exhausted with emotion, he was shipped
to Wimereux for a fortnight with a French teacher's
family who had advertised a vacancy. When this was
over and time was supposed to be at its healing work, he
returned to pick up his luggage for the new school year.
Tense and white-faced, he stood huddled among his bags
again on the station platform.

Edward, although he would have preferred to take him
this time by car, had decided that to break with custom
was itself a sort of danger. He eyed the boy uncertainly.

"Ah well, back among your friends soon, eh?" His
voice blaring with spurious cheer.

"I haven't got any."

"You'll see Venables," I reminded him.

The boy looked back at me bleakly. "He doesn't even know I'm there."

Unrequited love. So he too knows what it is.

The weeks are slipping away, in imitation of other years. The mornings are misty as before; the harvest moon has not broken with tradition. September is leading greyly and goldly into October, as it must have done since autumns first were. My shortened leg and my crooked back stiffen with rheumatism: they too are in keeping with seasonal custom. Acquaintances call or leave tactful messages. Condolences, deepest sympathy, always fresh flowers on the heaped earth, then the addition of headstone and marble kerb. Words, gestures; Megan still declaring she cannot believe it, Edward turning away his face.

I believe it, I understand. We shall not see Martine again. We and our memories are all of her that remain. She never knew she died. She was scarcely conscious even of living, but merely lived. That is the difference that keeps us apart. She came, and unheeding went on. We can never follow. Not by that route. However Megan tries, whatever stratagems she uses to persuade poor Edward to seek contact, there will be none. Martine is not a shade, but all light. Nothing holds her still to such as us.

It is useless, but they have asked me to be there. I will sit with them and we will link hands and wait. But *I know*. Useless.

*   *   *

Was it more cruel to let it happen than to have refused it in the first place? She expected so much. And Edward, what did he secretly hope for? His darling's voice, an echoed phrase from her Chopin Ballade? But that he had received already, one early summer evening as she played to me while he was away at Greenshards. Perhaps rightly the ghost-sounds belonged later, to this seance, and by some alchemy of love were transposed nearer in time to their physical source. But tonight there was nothing. Not a breath of wind, not a creaking board that an eager listener might have reshaped to fit his longings. At the table only Edward, Megan and the Fenwicks seemed real. Afterwards I couldn't recall having clearly seen the Blanchards at all. They were there of course, but I was not conscious of them. The links are broken. I no longer have this sense of a shared existence flowing between us, in and out of our several lives.

I noticed Giles only on the following evening when he called on Megan. She accepted his renewed regrets, not without a little stagey, exaggerated wildness. She pressed his hands in hers as though to comfort him in return. "We'll try it again," she promised.

"As often as you wish." And he looked long at me over her bowed head with a curious, new expression. Was it, I wonder, resentment?

I left them and went to find Edward. The study was empty, brown, acrid, like a dried-out walnut shell, on the desk an uncapped pen where ink had coagulated and scarred over the worn nib. His pipe lay there, cold and smoked-out. Hard ribs of ash showing he no longer troubled to clean it.

Those fine hands, so like my own, like Father's—Minton hands—had found a new lack of occupation. Always before moving gently, absorbedly, among papers, smoothing with appreciation textures of parchment, calf, briefly his children's hair, now they lay forever stranded and pallid on his knees, or under the desk lamp, severed from the dark shape of his body like some foreign matter washed up on the shore of the little pool of light. Edward unmoving, terribly alone, monstrously injured.

Tonight he wasn't there. Beyond the open window he made a slight movement on the terrace and I passed through to join him. A small moon covered us and the garden and the monochrome Victorian stucco with a vellum wash. I stood beside him and we were quiet together. At length I was sure it was all right to speak as I thought.

"There was another child," I reminded him. "The third one."

"The first."

Of course he was right. This one I spoke of had come before the others, before his marriage. This one, in time, was the first: (Martine had been the third.) A boy, he would be eighteen—no, nineteen—now. Noel, Edward's bastard. Mongoloid and sent away at birth.

"Is he...?" I asked.

Edward sighed. "He's still alive. At the same place. Father's arrangements still stand. After he died, I carried on. It's all taken care of in my will. If anything happens..."

He meant money. *Everything* taken care of; not really. Edward must have been thinking the same, for he moved wretchedly, then with an effort turned to me. "You've never spoken before..."

"I'd forgotten," I said truthfully. "It was such a very long time ago. And then, nobody knows."

"Except us."

And the child, of course. If he is capable of knowing anything.

"How—I mean—does he...?"

Edward's voice was stiff and muffled. "I've never seen him, except the once. The day he was born. I've never corresponded directly with the—place."

Perhaps someone should.

"All the papers about that are together in a file in the wall-safe. If ever you want to see them, you know where there's a key."

I didn't think at the time I should ever look for it, but within a matter of days I did, briefly, just to find the address.

Now that we had spoken, Edward seemed more normal. He began to exert himself more, but although his limbs were occupied, their movements were still those of an automaton. However, it was less distressing to see him brushing leaves from the lawns, or searching again among his documents instead of the endless, listless sitting in despair.

Megan, panting to resume the seances, insisted we should spend a neighbourly afternoon with the Blanchards by way of leading up to this, and although I would have preferred to stay free of them myself I went as some sort of protection for Edward.

The evening was almost uneventful, for Fenella had

a way of seeming able to forget whatever did not intimately concern her, and there was no constraint or deliberate avoiding of our family grief. We did for a few hours enjoy the quiet, grey melancholy of the October afternoon. Fenwick kept records quietly playing on the radiogram in the hall, and as the light failed slowly and the mist turned to drizzle we gazed out from armchairs in the firelit drawing-room and watched cattle slowly process, impassive under the rain, along the distant riverbank, while Bach fingered our minds with reasonable gentleness. *Metaphysiotherapy*, I remember saying half-aloud. And Edward smiled.

With the switching on of lamps there was no further point in leaving the windows uncovered. The reflecting panes were hooded with their velvet drapes. We stretched, rearranged our chairs and set ourselves to disposing of tea. Never had our neighbours seemed so normal, so un-Blanchard. Giles was common-place enough to consult Edward on the heating system at Greenshards.

"I'm sure I couldn't say," he parried some query. "I never lived here, you know." And he referred Giles to me.

In my throat I had the half-burning, half-constricted sensation of having run too fast—I, who only hobble. I kept my voice low and steady as I answered. But Giles was not interested in my reply. Bright-eyed, he leaned again towards Edward. "But your sister... Surely you—?"

"I have no sister," Edward told him. "Olive and I are cousins, only children of two brothers. That's how we came to live side by side. Uncle James took Greenshards

66

first, and later, when Olive's mother died, we came next-door."

"Aunt Ruth was a second mother to me," I said hurriedly, trying to cover with words—any that came to mind—the revelation Giles had unearthed.

He was not to be shaken off. "I was so sure you were brother and sister," he said. He turned again to me. "You think of yourself that way," he accused.

Some answer seemed expected of me. "Most of the time perhaps."

"There is nothing very special about sisters," complained Megan, sprawling by the flaming logs. "I had three, still have in fact. And two brothers."

"Six of you," said Fenella unexpectedly. "That must have been wild."

"Wild? In Welsh Wales, look you?" It pleased Megan to be puckish; she didn't normally care to be ribbed about her origins. "All very proper and Chapel twice-on-Sundays we were." She dropped the assumed Welsh accent and became ultra-English to prove how far she'd come. "Father was frightfully strict. I'd been acting two years in the West End before ever I dared to develop a temperament."

They were safely away on theatrical small-talk then and I could draw back into my chair and be forgotten.

But Fenella too let drop some revelations. She, it appeared, had also been for a short while on the stage, but what her line of entertainment was never came out, for not only was her husband quick to divert us to another topic but Megan, with the recognition of a rival in the same field, wasn't keen to pursue the question. Her own successes had been mainly in burlesque, and she would privately prefer to be thought a Bernhardt.

Before we left Greenshards Megan raised the question of a further seance. She put it to Giles, twisting her hands and looking from him to Fenella as though it were only a matter of their approval that stood between her and a glimpse of the dead child. I sensed Edward stiffen beside me and turned away, but Giles stared after me as I went. I felt his eyes as two wet fingers pressed on the nape of my neck. But I blundered on and reached here breathless. I have no idea what he has said to hold her off.

A disturbing evening. It is the day following the one we went to Greenshards. What the date is I cannot say, but it has been just such another grey, drizzly afternoon. A little after five-thirty I was here in this room. I came only for fresh table napkins from the hot-cupboard, but then I walked across to the window. That much I remember, and putting my finger out to touch the little hole low down in the lefthand pane. The sides were slippery and I had the sudden sensation of contracting and standing there, minute on the immense, treacherous slope while a great rush of air sucked me to the centre where the vortex screamed its way out and away. And then, still with this sense of being drawn, I thought I was walking, out in the rain. I wore my old beige Burberry, with knee boots, and my fingers were busy knotting a scarf under my chin. I put up one hand and felt, under its silk, the lacquered, bouffant shape of my hair that I'd had set that morning, and this persuaded me that I was really there, in fact walking through the steady drizzle, and away from Greenshards, not towards it.

I knew, and did not know, that this was Giles' doing. But why he should choose this way of exercising his influence I couldn't imagine. He knew we dined each night at seven thirty and that I was totally responsible for the meal. It meant, surely, that he would return me soon.

When I say that I thought this, it was a part of me only that was capable. The rest did blindly as he wished. And yet I was still able, had I chosen, to turn around and come back. I was curious. That was it. And so I allowed him to go on leading me in, like a small, helpless trout that cannot see the thread that plays him to the rod. Only, my part-that-was-apart was strong enough to recognise what happened, and it knew that wherever I went along this beamed path, there I should find Giles at its end. I knew, in fact, that I was being pulled, not sent.

At the end of the lane I turned off, (again away from Greenshards) towards the common, and I remarked objectively how although I made for some determined end which I couldn't name, yet I was able to get there by normal means, not by a straight bee-line as if I actually responded to some message such as radar. So I went, part automaton, part wondering at the mechanics of it all. And so I came out on the railway footpath, above the clearing where the down-line from London leaves the Addiscombe tunnel.

For one mad moment I thought he might be making me throw myself on the line, and the brief second of horror so shook my mind that the link was shattered and for whole minutes I stood there shivering in the rain, feeling myself on the verge of damnation. Everything I saw was distorted, alien. And then slowly the customary pattern of things reasserted itself. The leprous hand spreading over the embankment below swam apart, resolved itself into a mildewed stain, then took on depth and became separate, lichen-marked boulders tumbled on the tussocky slope. The silver ganglion-mass of fibres netting the path ahead sorted themselves into a clump of birches, each tree normal, with its own branches and a single trunk. The boiling of clouds withdrew again behind gentle rain, and down the track drifted a wisp of wood-smoke where they burned hedging trash before the limits of the station. Out of the quiet of the autumn evening came the rumble of a train in the Addiscombe tunnel.

I had so often in the past watched from up here and then gone unseen away. Such a familiar thing to be doing. When Father had been due home from London. Or when I was impatient for Edward's return. It hardly seemed possible that now I did it under Giles' command. It must somehow have become mixed in with a suppressed wish of my own. It was I who intended to come here then, and my mind was transferring responsibility on to Giles?

I crouched on my heels, with my head against the stranded wire that lined the path, and I looked down into the tunnel. So long, reaching so far back, having such deep shadows, it seemed to mean far more than it physically was. It became time past, and half-forgotten fears; it was separation; it was all the long corridors of

nightmare met in one. And then light came curving
along it, transforming it into the normal, then the comfortable, then the desirable. It wasn't separation any
more, but communion.

The rails had taken up that curious ringing of wheels
almost upon them. I stood up again and I leaned forward,
determined to see what about this particular train should
have such compulsive power over me.

And then it burst from the opening, roaring, and
churning into the dusk, whipped up with its rush of air
an old newspaper discarded by the track, that flapped
and turned over and flew to embrace it, ardently pressing
itself against a square yellow window. I felt myself,
equally discarded, suddenly taut, passionate, snatched
up and with it thrusting at some desired one within. And
there, half-turned at a window, looking directly up at me
on the slope, stood Giles.

With the lighted carriage behind him and the evening
mists shadowing the entire embankment, he could not
have seen me. *Should* not have. And it would have been
equally impossible for me to have seen his face, for the
whole of him should have been a black silhouette. And
yet I saw distinctly every feature. I saw the expression of
weary satisfaction as he somehow contacted me out there
in the dark.

The slowing train moved on like the trailed half of an
incandescent worm. I heard its brakes go on.

There it has stopped, people are getting out. I can't see
them, beyond the curve in the track, down at the station.
Doors are slamming, footsteps reverberate along the
hollow platform. But I mustn't think of the indeter-

minate passengers greyly passing into the grey mist. Fix my mind on one, on Giles.

Giles, that's it. Here is the thread again. I go on. Down to the station? Almost certainly. Ah, he is there waiting, his car under the skeleton of a lime tree. The door on my side is open.

I climbed in, and at once he put the car in gear. We sat without speaking until he stopped again, halfway down the combe. He switched off the ignition, but there was still a strange singing tone that went on. At last he spoke.

"What are you afraid of?" he demanded. "Was it so much to ask?"

I sat on in silence, not completely sure for once what he was expecting of me.

"I hadn't dreamed," he said, trying again, "that you felt such resentment of your cousin's wife."

"I don't resent—"

"And yet you won't help her. Instead you sit there and with all your ugly determination baulk her attempts—"

He shouldn't have said that. Not *ugly*! Ah, Giles, how that hurts!

He knew immediately what he had done and swept me in close, holding me fiercely. I could hear the fear in his heartbeats.

"Not you. I don't mean you," he whispered. "It's just defiance that's so ugly. Never you, Olive. How could you think I meant that?"

Suddenly I discovered we were making love. I had to stop and there were wretched accusations. He did not quite understand that I was only part-dominated then.

Or perhaps he intended to leave me some sliver of free choice and relied upon his passion to override that. But it didn't. I couldn't go on.

It wasn't prudery. It wasn't any calculating balance of opportunism. No attempt to extract promises or receipts. I just couldn't.

He was desperate. "No," I kept saying. "No, Giles, no!" And all the time he went on fighting me. With his hands and his mind.

"Olive, why? Can't you admit we belong?"

I could barely speak, my teeth were so tightly clenched. "I want you," I managed to say, "but I can't. There's something, a block. I—was raped as a child."

What made me say that? No wish of mine, no pre-meditation certainly. And just as certainly it hadn't sprung from his mind, for he faced me in horror, his face gleaming wet from my rain-soaked scarf and skin.

As I sit here writing I still feel his fingers biting into my arms. I can hear my own voice calling out, and the words I spoke. And although I can't believe them, yet I know that it's true. Like Megan, I suppose, knowing Martine is dead and still unable to believe it. For I *was* raped as a child. That is sure, and it is just as sure that in some strange and protective way I had completely managed to forget it until now. Forget a thing like that? How little we know ourselves. And I so proud of my intellectual honesty!

Megan has just come tapping at the door. Fenella phoned half an hour ago. They have arranged a seance for Thursday evening. Reluctantly I have agreed to be there. That is four days away. Perhaps something will happen to prevent my having to go. I hope so. But if I must be there, I have made up my mind, I shall neither help nor make it harder. It is their business, the Blanchards' and the Fenwicks'. I shall take no part, one way or the other.

6

THE FOUR DAYS since that meeting have seemed empty, because Giles has neither appeared nor sent any message to bring me across to him. It is strange, as I brush my hair each morning or set on my hideous, proper little hat to go out, I look at the calm old-fashioned spinster in the mirror and marvel at what the casing covers.

He has given me these days of grace before I declare myself. But declare myself as what? His creature, I suppose. And why not? Isn't he, after all, the only person who has ever guessed at the true nature underneath? Not *guessed*, no; none of Giles' knowledge is mere guesswork. But he recognises the essence of me, the unused, ardent energy that I have denied even to myself—particularly to myself. He has given me four days to admit to myself what I am, to recognise myself for the first time ever.

I saw this only dimly. The whole period was a dim phase for me, lit with brief flashes of insight into incidentals that did not personally concern me. I went about the trivial business of the day, planned meals, shopped for and prepared them, served them and saw to their clearing away. I ensured, half-attending, that the house and all in it was, like my own exterior, seemly and ordered. And then at some utterly ordinary moment I would have knowledge of some other moment in the still-future and in it myself looking back to this one again. And recognising it as meaningful. But for what? What have I now in my hands, or almost comprehended? Just a different relationship of time that appears to make one insignificant moment sublime, almost immortal. A concept of time set in a sort of circle, but with another limitless dimension.

Or I would be struck motionless bending over the emptying bath while my damp body grew chill and I read galaxies and universes into the stirring soap scum that floated, moving separately and also together, form-ing almost-pattern yet never in any existence capable of exact repetition. And it was marvellous to be part of a similar creation, a diminutive speck within a speck, shar-ing in a common consciousness and yet able to think and act and feel, the *whole* of me now a part apart.

It is the same whether I watch soapy water flowing steadily away, or touch the intricate, unique design of frost fixed to my window, or at night marvel how the sky is awhirl with stars. The meaning is the same, each whole organised, but so diffusely that we see only the great overall motion of the hierarchy and call it natural law. And having given it a name, we consider that is all, and cease to think.

In the beginning was not the word, but an idea. It is in accepting a word that we have lost the idea. But it is out there somewhere, and it exists as a germ in the smallest division of the smallest part of each atom. There is no end to scale, for I conceive of the lesser everlastingly within the less, and conversely the greater forever containing the great. (But in that direction it is harder to comprehend. And yet it's still true.)

And then the moment of revelation is gone (like the bath water) and I am cold and must cover my ugly form with clothes and go about my inconsequential affairs.

I took the car into Bensons' to have the steering checked. They run the place like an operating theatre; each case has its appointment time and a clip of papers covering the progress of the disease. While it was there I shopped, including the usual Turkish Delight for old Mr. Blackstock. His house, like an Edwardian water-works, blank with a lofty elegance, backs on to the lane where Edward has his chambers, although the front stares out from its over-tall windows across fields to Long Barrow in the west. I used to visit there sometimes as a child and wait for Uncle Arthur to pick me up in his fearsome Lagonda. Mr. Blackstock was old even then and our excuse for calling had been that his housekeeper was once Edward's nursemaid before he went to school. Now she organises the child in a senile old man and the motive for my regular call, mixed with nostalgia admittedly, is occasionally to referee the unequal contest of the two failing relics.

I put the little round box in his shrivelled, reptilian claw. When the woman had drawn his attention to it he felt it uncertainly, recognised the shape and texture and nodded, making little toothless gasps.

"Say 'Thank you' to the lady," shouted the ageing dragon.

"Ah?" he resisted.

They would go on like that for hours if I allowed them.

I noticed she had had his television repaired again. It had been his custom, when he was more nimble with the wheelchair, to go straight across while the mechanic was barely out of the house and drive the machine—there was no other way to describe his manipulations—until the picture was a sheet of whirling snow against a crackle of static. Originally he must have been trying to improve reception: his motives had never been deliberate destruction. But so angry did he become at his own maladroitness and his housekeeper's scoldings that he would declare eventually he preferred the screen that way. Mrs. Mullins had never discovered that at some later point his statement became neither more nor less than the simple truth. Had she been less preoccupied with his increasing physical debility she might have observed how confused the advertised programmes made him, while the test cards gave only slight relief. Even they demanded of him more than he was able to offer. The geometrically arranged oblongs and circles, the eternal, unknown child smirking back at him while she waited to draw on her blackboard, baffled him. Was he expected to do something with this puzzle of shapes? Should he recognise the child? There were so many little girls about now and all exactly alike, pert and knowing and always up to something. Some niece's child, or grandniece's; he had lost count what they were now. He needed something to look at while he sat and remembered and he didn't want it moving about too much, but if a picture stayed the same it worried him almost as much. All in all it was better when the snow started covering the screen and it crackled like a good fire under a spitted pig. Made him think of winters when he was a boy; they were more real than young women howling into clutched microphones or railway trains rushing right out of the cabinet at you.

"I've 'ad 'is set put right again," Mrs. Mullins said proudly, plunging her hands into her cardigan pockets and then winding them upwards one over the other until the woolly thing was a sort of lumpy tube rolled across her waist. In just this way she used to crumple her starched white apron when she prepared to 'have it out with one of what she considered 'the gentry'.

"It went right off again straight after you called last time."

I looked at old Mr. Blackstock and wondered if he were capable of having betrayed me. But he sat on, open-mouthed, a yard from the screen and planted square in the path of a galloping stallion. From inside his paralysis he fought back feebly.

"Maybe I have an adverse effect on these things," I suggested. "It might be wiser to turn it off till I've gone."

She did so, her own eyes still mesmerised by the little electronic tyrant. As it clicked and the rectangle of light dwindled down the tube, the old man gave a small choking gasp and all the resistance went out of him. As far as his dried-up, turtle mouth was able he gave a sort of smile.

"There," she said, " 'e's like the set, see? 'Is light goes out just the same."

I opened the box of Rahat Lacoum and popped a soft little cube of the pink stuff—the rose-flavoured kind—

between Mr. Blackstock's waiting jaws, then I offered
the box to Mrs. Mullins. When she went for her inevitable offering of home-made quince jam I put my hand
behind the cooling set and twiddled every knob I could
find.

Mrs. Mullins pushed in her trolley laid with the tea
things. I had to endure more condolences on Martine,
and another display of Mr. Blackstock's sucking at the
saucer held against his lips.

"*Now!*" she would give him the word each time she
had it tilted to her satisfaction. I remembered how, with
the same word, she had trained the young Edward to
blow his nose. And he had been quite a big boy then,
eight or nine. She always said that I, three years behind
him, had been born knowing how to use a handkerchief.

At last I was free to go. Mrs. Mullins gave up fussing
over the crumbs powdering the wrinkles of the old man's
waistcoast and started checking up on me. Both gloves?
One right, the other left. That was all right then.

"Just let him have his telly back," she said, stabbing
it on before steering me to the door, and I delayed her
there long enough for the set to warm up. When I re-
crossed his window he sat facing a blank rectangle of
light diagonally traversed by a set of telegraph wires. I
hadn't done too badly; at least he was free of B.B.C. and
I.T.V. Now he could tune to his own private wavelengths.
I left him to more relevant programmes.

On the surface, a routine domestic, vaguely do-goodish
sort of day. Much the same as life before the Blanchards
came. The main difference being that then I should
never have dared to interfere with Mrs. Mullins' arrange-

ments. I should not, for that matter, have seen any point in it. But I have learnt a lot about communication in the past six months. Mr. Blackstock has not much more of life to live. He has the right to sort it out in his own, rambling fashion. Without interference.

Next morning, in the Public Library, I only just avoided a face-to-face with the Vicar. Not that I object to him in any way, but meeting again so soon after the funeral could have embarrassed us both. He has done his official duty by the family, expressed the ritual condolences. Underneath all that he may be a little ashamed of his god. The Common Prayer has been revealed as short of comfort; anything he could remember to quote would sound merely academic, and he has enough sense to know it. This time his god has failed to provide the alternative ram in a thicket. But perhaps I do the Rev. Irvine Reynolds an injustice. He is strong on chastity, mediaeval vestments and the Easter Offering, but not the supernatural. It is, after all, vaguely improper to imagine him believing in a god at all.

Edward came home with a dog inside his coat. Not a puppy; it is about a year old and housetrained. Some clients of his are going abroad and want it to join a family who would care for it. He presented it to me, personally, a little embarrassed for fear I should think it some clumsy attempt to provide a substitute for the missing child. It is an engaging little beast. But it wouldn't do to become attached—I shall have to ask Edward to find it another home.

On Friday I looked up the address of the institute where Noel is kept. I explained by phone that I was on my way, and then I had no excuse to evade it.

The place is a little beyond Salisbury, and, for what it is, not too alarming in aspect. There are trees, but even outdoors there is a cleared-way, aseptic look as though the very fields are carefully watched. There is nowhere left to hide except in oneself.

They had arranged for me to meet him in a special room, a wax-polished box emptied of dangers. Everything in it that might be straight is cautiously rounded, like the corners of old Mr. Blackstock's illuminated screen, smoothed off so that he shall not clumsily bruise on them the arthritic edges of his softening mind. I asked instead to see the boy wherever he happened to be, normally occupied and among others like him.

There was some consultation over this and I intercepted the eyebrow messages. After so many years of neglect, any insistence on sounding the atmosphere must appear unsuitably sensitive. But they had the habit of humouring; for that I am grateful.

We went into a larger room carpeted with serviceable brown haircord. There were curtains, patterned in blue and greens pulled back from a huge, square window set with many oblong panes in such a way that you scarcely saw the iron bars, painted to match the cream woodwork behind them. Over this whole expanse of glass the rain bleakly poured so that it seemed we were in some recess behind a waterfall. But the room faces south; they assured me of that. So whenever possible he does have sunshine.

These were the things I saw last, of course, while I could not say anything, only words inside myself, deliberately, to occupy my mind, force it to follow physically my eyes, note, list, measure, assess, be practical. What I saw first, all that I saw, was the group of little humans on the floor.

I knew at once which was Noel, for the woman in the floral smock—they weren't dressed as nurses—went to him as soon as she saw me come in. She bent over him as he sat absorbed in a plastic yacht that floated in the bay of his legs. She whispered and he looked up at her, smiling with his mouth open. She spoke again and he bobbed his head.

He started to get up, remembered the toy and turned back for it. Then he stood and let her lead him to me. Tall, more sturdy than his father at that age, but with those same vulnerable, elongated wrists of youth like Edward's when he had sired him. Minton bones, but with a difference, the neck forward thrusting, the head —all wrong. The whole face was rested and slack except for the eyebrows where a terrible struggle went on. The open mouth gaped in greeting. He spoke.

"Mother. Mother?" At least, I think it was that, and the woman in the floral smock smiled and nodded as though he was her prize pupil. His eyes went over me vaguely and back to her. And he turned away. It was only a word. Not one they used very often here.

The matron was understanding. That is to say she was kind and forgave. She went as far towards understanding as was possible across so great a gulf fixed between us. She poured tea, showed me reports—but did not insist I read them—repeated a few simple sentences until she was certain that their message had reached me: that he was better here, good with the smaller ones, gentle usually, and at other times his fury could soon be deflected.

Was there anything he wanted? She thought not. The simpler the life the better. They have, she said, their own compensations. At times he was radiantly happy.

I shall never tell Edward I have seen him.

The simpler the life the better, she said. Mine has been too complicated for me. I have had to tell lies to cover the truth, and even that was not enough. I have had to make myself believe them too. And now I am more deformed as a person than I have ever dared to admit myself in body.

Calling love rape. And then forcing forgetfulness on top of that.

Sick as I am and now see myself to be, yet I am thankful I came. But he should not have said what he did. Poor child. It is a word I am not ready for.

7

IN THIS STATE I submitted to the seance. Giles seemed disturbed at my appearance but I assured him I would not wilfully obstruct. If any of the others found my manner strange they would have attributed this to the same strain they were under themselves.

I do not remember the night, whether there was a moon or not, nor whether it rained. Perhaps it had turned cold, for Edward insisted on transporting us from door to door in the car. We were offered no food or drink at Greenshards, but simply walked into the hall and sat straight down at the table. We had met because of Martine, so it was on her that I tried to fix my mind, and we waited a long time in silence. Then—it was as though I was permitted to live again what had gone. In the space of a few minutes she was reborn and grew. I rocked her in my arms, I told her stories by the fire, we sewed together and she pricked her thumb, I saw again her first attempts at swimming and twisted my fingers through the shoulder straps of her costume, terrified lest she sink. I made her a party dress and trimmed it with pink silk curled into little rosebuds; I watched her fail at the gymkhana and held her close when she sobbed with frustration. All this, and then I watched her face change, slacken, the mouth hang open. Her lively hair shrank off her and left a curiously rounded head on a forward-thrusting neck. I fought to dismiss Noel's blunt features, heard myself cry out, started half-awake, opened my eyes. And I looked down the table from the wrong position, saw and recognised the others as they sat there, hands linked, watching me: Edward, Mrs. Fenwick, Giles, Megan, Fenwick and the other woman.

The other woman. I looked again. It was Olive Minton. She was fast asleep.

I cried out in fear and she woke up, the beginnings of alarm in her face too. But by then I was travelling fast across the table towards her. She seemed to struggle with incomprehension and then I—she—yes, *I* was back in my place, looking, with the others, down to where Fenella sat moaning and tugging with both hands at her gold and enamel collar.

Mrs. Fenwick leaned forward. "That's enough," she whispered. "You've done so well. Fenella, wake up."

And then in that brief instant of sensing, and resenting, the unfairness of what she said, I acknowledged what had till then seemed impossible.

Giles suddenly unlinked hands, breaking the circle, and leaned over to touch me. He knew. But of course he knew, for that was what he had always intended. Giles, if anyone, would acknowledge that his wife was no more than a ventriloquist's doll. I—Olive Minton or something from inside her—had replaced Fenella. I was the true sensitive, able to project myself and communicate beyond the physical limits, and Fenella no more than the vacuum I had used to pass through.

She was pleased with herself, although she had no more idea than I what message or experiences the others had received. Their gratitude, however, was evidence that the seance was some kind of success, though Megan was already pressing for more. "Now that we've established a link," she begged, "can't we go on? I must be sure she's all right wherever she is. Happy. Oh, please."

"Megan, no!" Edward insisted. It had been as much as he could bear, poor man. I felt his pain twisting inside me. He had been with his darling Marty a while: that was enough. He would need time now to accept or refute it. Whichever way it went with him he would suffer.

"Let us go home," I said. I might not exist for all the notice they took of my voice. I walked back alone, leaving them still pressing about Fenella. Later, as I sat here by the window in the linen-room, I heard the car come back, high heels cross the hall below, the sound of the garage doors, Edward's slow tread on the stairs.

It is their life, their choice. She was their child. But I know there will never be a message, not the way they want. If tonight they heard her voice it was an echo of what has been, gathered from our joint consciousness, condensed, distilled (or whatever the physical imagery of the phenomenon may be), and projected through me. I have no contact with her now, only memory, and that grows less. The innocent dead do not return. They have no need.

The window is my mirror. Again the world outside is black, quite gone, and all that exists is this lighted room with its fixed, unmoving picture. I see something known as Olive Minton that stares back at me with alien eyes. Her I know of, but who am *I*? Giles is calling me. I am conscious of his demands, like the thin thread of wind that enters by the hole in the glass, that navel-round fault he uses to feed, and feed on, my mind. I shall not come. There are greater mysteries here, facing me.

I am. But *who* am I? This is the verge of horror, the beginning of wisdom.

Giles has spoken of exorcising ghosts. How strange that he should wish to do that when ostensibly he has been co-operating in something that is almost the opposite. But he doesn't see the inconsistency. I have told him that Martine will not return and that I can never reach her now. He tried to persuade me otherwise and it struck me that although he has read and studied a great deal about such matters, he actually knows little more than I do myself. He wished to impose his will on mine (this will-power that he doesn't care to acknowledge!) but I have insisted that in this I know, and so now he accepts that it is so. He will plead some specious reason for not continuing the seances: Fenella's health perhaps, and the strain upon her constitution! But whatever the excuse, that is the right decision, for Edward's sake if not my own. And Giles would not care to have the attempts tail away and become a laughing-stock. He has, I think, some idea of how vindictive Megan might become if her mania were further excited without ultimate satisfaction.

As for the exorcising, I think there too he refers to a non-existent ghost. For he is convinced my mind is trammelled by the memories of something that never actually happened: the rape I once spoke of. He speaks in terms of liberating the full potential of my mind and

I listen gravely, almost gratefully, to this jargon of traumatic scars and true integration of the personality.

I too am learning a little of the jargon from an extraordinary book I chanced upon. It was when I contrived to avoid the Rev. Irvine Reynolds in the Public Library. I moved away into a bay of books that I'd had no occasion to look through before. At that moment I took no notice of what I buried my nose in, but on leaving I had been pressed for time and mistakenly took this book with me.

It is an account by an American doctor of a series of cases of dissociated personality. Just the reverse of what Giles refers to as 'true integration'. It seems to me that this is what actually happens in Fenella's case, that she becomes in a way dissociated or absent. I, on the other hand, who also 'take trips away', am active rather than passive when this happens. I intend to read a little more on the subject and seek out some sound authorities before I tackle Giles upon this. I need to be able to stand my ground with a certain amount of background knowledge. He can be very persuasive.

We met tonight and he began the exorcism. He is a very accomplished and delicate lover. Fenella sat near us, 'asleep', as he performed the rites. She would certainly have cause to fear me now, if she knew. Perhaps the knowledge will leak to her, as other of my thoughts have done before; but even then what can she do? No one would ever believe her. They have only to look at her beauty and then at me. Who could be persuaded that poor Olive Minton would contemplate even so briefly taking Fenella's place?

89

Now Edward and Megan, in their own ways, have set about forgetting. Giles has persuaded them that already they have received more than it is normally granted to a human mind to know and Martine must be allowed to go her way alone. And, left behind, they begin to bicker, at almost senile level. But at least it is communication. And now there are more rehearsals and filming to take Megan back to London. She complains, but she will go, with something approaching relief. Edward will work a little harder, a little longer, in order not to spend too much time dwelling on Martine, because it may hold her back from what is truly hers. He will not admit he accepts this notion, but he will observe its requirements, just in case. He is the same about walking under ladders, always finding some way to avoid deliberately avoiding them.

I find myself more and more in the company of the dog. It is an amiable creature, a dachshund; sharp, round, square, but not of course all at the same time. There are sharp days when it is all stretched, questing nose and quivering tail, ears cocked, whiskers abristle; round days when it lies, kidney-curved and bladder-soft in its circular, plastic and sponge-rubber bed; four-square days with legs planted wide, boxy and sturdily defiant, forever presenting its impudent hindquarters like some cubist dartboard covered in a short-haired pelt. But I must not become involved or dependent on an animal. I have told Edward he must look elsewhere to find it a home. He thinks I am worried at it not getting sufficient exercise, and has offered it to Giles. Fenella, however, cannot stand dogs and has flatly refused to take it. Now he is thinking of approaching one of his clients. I hope it will go soon.

Already it is December. Andrew is due to return from school next week and then Christmas will be upon us before we know.

I have followed former practice, preparing mincemeat, puddings, the iced fruit cake, ordered turkey, nuts, dates, tangerines, *marrons glacés* and all the hollow trimmings. But activity is not enthusiasm. I fear the empty days of huddling together indoors, a family that isn't any more. For Andrew, as Edward insists, we must make it appear the same as ever. But why? Is it such an admirable thing to show him how adept we are at lying?

Snow came as a final horror, when already we had enough with gifts and carols and sleights of memory. I could never have called the child Noel if I had foreseen. And when I gave him that evocative name, I was still a child myself. I had never heard the word mongol, nor seen what it was. My son had been born on Christmas Eve in my sixteenth year, and I had thought they were going to let me keep him. I believed Uncle Arthur had chosen a London nursing home for greater efficiency, and no one explained that once my baby came the secret still must go on. It has gone on till now.

Edward and I remember but say nothing. He sees the small, red-faced monster he was compelled by his father to face. (Uncle Arthur always believed in accepting responsibility for one's own actions. Yet he never let me see the baby.) The child I remember is a young adult, as its father was when we loved, but without his beauty, his essence. Edward, slipping home from Cambridge in term time to meet me in the summer garden of Greenshards, where I crept at night by way of the gap in the green beech hedge—it seemed the hedge was never brown then —and slid as secretly back to my room at dawn, drenched with dew and heady love. Our baby, when I knew it had begun, was to have been an Apollo.

Giles is puzzled. Assiduously as he works at his exorcism, the gap between us remains. Only briefly do we possess each other and when it is over what is there? —I am alone again. Some other ghost, he says, is there in my mind.

I will not let him dominate me entirely, for fear of what he may find out, and yet this game of cat and mouse cannot last for ever. I must submit at length, because he is right. There is a ghost, though not that of a non-existent rape. Nor will he discover my early love, for he is looking for guilt and in that there was none.

My ghost is there and I see it dimly; its outline is taking on a strangely familiar shape. It is ugly with fear and ancient superstitions, and—yes, he was right—with guilt.

And now he knows; he is satisfied. This afternoon he asked to see the room I spent so much of my time in and I brought him up here, curious to see what he would make of it. He looked around at the plaster walls; the doors behind which I stack the laundered sheets and towels; the bare wood floor; the mahogany chest of drawers that is too old-fashioned to go elsewhere but still has capacious depths for linen; its tilted mirror, damp-spotted; my cane chair; the little splinter-hole in the lower lefthand pane of the window.

"Where do you keep your manuscript?" he asked me. "In there?" and he pointed to the cupboard where the highest stack of sheets is stored.

I nodded.

He went across to the window and bent above its ledge. "Look," he said, "a perfect prism. See how the light outside is caught and broken into its elements of colour."

I moved across after him and stared where he now pointed. I saw the window and the little pitted hole.

"Look closer," he insisted.

And then, only a few inches from my eyes there was a pure rainbow. I saw the light dissolve and the colours emerge, and then in terms of light I saw how my self could dissolve and take on separate shades that flowed outwards and then merged and became light again in some other persona. I heard myself tell him all this while the spectrum danced on the edge of the glass crater and light became colour became light again and then was indistinguishable from all the other mass of light that had no beginning, no end, and was everywhere.

"And when something comes between," he said softly, "What then?"

I stared at the little crater of glass and understood. "There is a shadow. The colours have all gone," I told him. I went on looking at the shadow and the darkness grew, took on the familiar outline that yet I hadn't quite recognised. "It is my father," I said. "He killed himself because of me." And my voice went on, and I heard questions put and myself answering, and all the time it was as though part of me, the greater, feeling part relived that terrible time in my childhood when I was injured because he crashed the car and then, appalled at the disfigurement he'd caused, he killed himself, killed me in him, but never him in me. And all through it the guilt was reflected an eternity of times, like a candle's image thrown between mirrors until it was numberless and everywhere and there was no escaping it. Guilt, because he thought himself responsible for what happened to me, and so I was responsible for what he did to himself. And though he chose to drive when he did, yet the reason for his bursts of grief and the drinking they brought on was me, growing every day more like my mother and every day farther from him.

All this I told Giles and asked him, "Shall I forget it again when I awake?" And he kissed my face and said, "You will remember it all now, even asking me that. And you are not asleep, so open your eyes."

I opened them, and the first thing I saw was the window, with the small, cratered hole where Andrew had once fired an airgun pellet through, by accident from the garden. And I saw that there was no direct sunlight anywhere, for it was a cold, overcast day and the first few snowflakes of a fresh fall were starting.

It snowed gently all evening and then cleared for a starry night. I sat for many hours, looking out at the whiteness of moonlight on the whiteness of snow and all was surgically smooth and cured. There was no more rainbow and the shadows were black and solid and they reminded me of no one.

When at last I went to bed it was to dream. I was walking again across the common in my raincoat and knee boots, knotting the scarf under my chin as I hurried. It was as though I was going again to meet Giles at the station, but events of the past day had woven themselves in, for instead of rain it was a starlit night and the ground was covered with several inches of crisp snow. Although I tried to run—I had not sloughed off my deformity in the dream—I was barely in time to see the train light the outer edges of the Addiscombe tunnel. I stood on the footpath above and heard the pounding of the wheels lessen as the brakes were applied for the stop, saw the chain of square, yellow windows stream out into the black of the cutting, saw figures within waiting near doors, lifting down cases, saw suddenly in close-up as if a pair of fieldglasses had been put before my eyes—my father, older than in his lifetime, look up towards me and smile.

Then the night was abruptly broken with the squealing, shuddering impact of the crash as first the engine and then the two following coaches left the rails and ploughed straight on into the grassy bank. A terrible rending as later coaches ran into the settling ones, splintering them into crumpled straw, two jack-knifing upwards, erect an instant and then toppling towards the flames that flared briefly along the track's side and hissed to nothing in the snow.

Breathless from the speed with which I'd come, I could only cling to a post at the height of the embankment. Five strands of wire barred me from getting down, but even had I pulled them apart and thrust myself through I could never have managed the steep slope in that snow, for at parts it is sheer drop. But already there were lights showing below, figures coming running with torches, shouts, and somewhere somebody screaming. I started hobbling down the path towards the station and when I reached it there was no one there. The ticket office had been closed since the last train up at ten fifteen and now the only men on duty had run up the line to the crash. I had to sit on a trolley to stop my heart from hammering so, and I was still there in a state of some shock when the doctors arrived from the cottage hospital.

They said no one was seriously hurt, just a matter of keeping a few people in overnight while they made quite sure the injuries were superficial.

By now I knew it was no dream but really happening, for there were no surrealist inconsistencies—only the impossibility of my father having been there. There was no one, they told me, in the restaurant car where I'd seen him. I had to believe them; they were all local men and knew he had been dead for over twenty years. What could I tell them that they would accept?

Someone gave me a lift home in a car, and since the house was in darkness I came in quietly so that Edward never knew I had been out. I lay again in bed and told myself that if Father had been in that coach he would have been killed, for it was the one that splintered to pieces. He would be dead; and was dead anyway. Then I understood why he had looked so old, at least twenty years older, for this was the time that he would have died had he not tampered with his own life span. At least this time he had smiled up at me before he had to die. And it no longer mattered that he had killed himself, for tonight's death had now cancelled it out.

I slept, and if I dreamt, at least I never recalled the dream.

By noon next day the snow had begun to thaw, then a sea wind roared up with the dark. It buffeted the garden and stripped off the last shreds of sterile dressing. The world went back to rotting, sweetly, dankly, under a beech-brown mush.

On New Year's Eve Giles came across, in person, to say how Fenella was to die.

8

A CLOCK STRIKES, but only the half—adrift from the hours that make sense of it. How many have already gone?

This is an unknown station in the night, echoing and empty. A single shout—a foreign voice—harsh boots of the Customs men on the clanking platform; coach springs audibly relax; someone taps a wheel and it goes on ringing, all along the rail, forever in a tunnel of time. Half-awake I recall Vallorbe, the night train to Milano. The Swiss border with France: half a night yet to go, half a journey, half a lifetime. Go to sleep again. When Italy arrives you will wake up, still seventeen, going adventuring, the world ahead open and beckoning.

But I can't make that dream come back. I can only stop the bad ones, not recapture the good ones that have gone. There is no point in sleep without dreams. My body is not tired, but my mind—I need to think. So much to think out that I must use the night as well. So little time left.

If I die all will have stopped. Springs and Summers, children in parks, trees, bright leaves blowing along paths, roses, kites, woodsmoke, fountains, laughter, frost. It's not enough that for others they will still exist. There will be nothing of me left; nor anyone to remember me; no child of mine as a claim on the future, for Noel is frozen into an endless present, like some curious fossil trapped in a glacier. To die is the destruction of the whole world.

I have now existence only in myself, in the persona of Olive Minton, inside this deformed body.

If anyone says, 'Olive Minton? Ah, yes,' they are seeing deformity, not my hair or my hands. It is as though I had never mind, nor eyes nor breasts nor thighs but am only a twisted spine and a shortened leg that ends in a clumsy surgical boot. I could have been beautiful and loved. I could have made others happy by simply existing. Instead, I have had to work hard to keep them merely comfortable and well-mannered to me and adequately fed. All that I love of life is beauty. Shouldn't I too have had a little?

Across at Greenshards Fenella lies awake. Her room is on the far side so there is no show of light, but I know. She sleeps fitfully and has frightening dreams. Her neurologist has been down from London to see her and prescribed sleeping pills. Giles looks after them for fear she should take too many. She wants to be dead, because she is afraid of dying. It sounds a terrible confusion, but I understand. She knows it will be soon, and even while she tries to run away, she wishes it were already over. It makes a near-imbecile of her by day, but she is still beautiful.

I have been Fenella for a while, and I was beautiful then. And I was needed. Through me, in Fenella, they had Martine again. When Fenella finally goes, I shall be in her place.

The light from my window falls across the angles of the roof and catches the corner of the drawing-room chimney. Up here in the linen-room I am the only one awake in this house. Megan is away again and Edward sleeps heavily after a long evening's work in the study. Andrew is young and resilient enough, even under all that anger, barely to crease his sheets at night. His anger was sudden and surprised me with its violence, for he had been so quiet and negative over Christmas. But when Sammy Crowther arrived Andrew went straight out of the house and was not seen until evening. Then he came to me as I set the dinner table, his fists bunched and his body rigid.

"Why don't you do something?" he demanded. "Doesn't Father know what they're up to?"

"Perhaps he doesn't want to know," I answered.

"Is that your attitude too? Just close your eyes to it? You could stop it, say something."

"Look, Andrew," I said, "it's none of my business." (Nor really of his, though it could have such far-reaching effects on his own circumstances.) "I'm not prepared to upset the whole household for the sake of confirming or refuting what's only a conjecture—"

"What sort of proof do you want then?" he demanded. "You can see as well as I do what's going on."

"Not in this house," I argued. "Whatever you suppose happens elsewhere, I assure you that here—"

"Only because they don't get the chance. You could at least speak to my mother. The man's detestable!"

Poor boy. He wants to identify himself with Edward, but thinks him spineless and therefore despicable. Which makes the boy ashamed. And does he suspect, in his confusion, that really he is jealous? We all have a little touch of Oedipus. But to him that is only an ancient idea bound inside the covers of a classbook. In time he will grow up. Perhaps he has begun, because he looked away for a while, then came round the table and eyed me levelly. "I think I know why you're not making any fuss. It's not the first time, is it?"

I said nothing, which was an answer in itself. He stood behind my turned back a moment, and then went quietly away. He has said nothing since, but he burns inside. I think he will be glad to go back to school on Thursday. There is more, perhaps, that I should have said, but he measures all in terms of loyalties. Marriage is more than that. He is too young to see that Megan has been generous as a wife, even as a lover. She gave Edward life, gaiety, a flashpoint his steady-burning devotion would otherwise never have known. Perhaps the boy would be ashamed that in fact his father is still grateful.

The dog has gone. Edward gave him in the end to Mrs. Mullins, who is nervous of strangers coming to the door. A queer household for such a lively little animal, but she will feed it well, baby it, and there are the fields for it to run free in. Now that Andrew has gone I have only Edward and Giles left in my world. And Fenella, of course. There is still Fenella.

And I. Whoever *I* may be.

It used to seem more simple. 'I' was a compound of memories and attitudes, no more one person than any of us is, but functioning on many levels of consciousness. We all know what it is to sit back while another part of us performs. And at times we act automatically, our brain minimally involved while we think quite deeply of something unrelated. All of that is normal, habitual. But this *being someone* is a terrifying thing, for when we peer inside, there is so much complex activity, so many distinct shapes of personalities at work, pulling against each other, flowing together and then apart, that I remember the stars and the Milky Way, and the marvellous nebulae of soap scum moving on the face of the water, and I see myself so.

I have made a new discovery and gained from it a new freedom and a new subjection. It was when I was in Greenshards last evening.

Edward and I had been invited across after dinner and we were sitting there, the two men smoking and talking quietly from time to time. I looked at Giles as he slouched in one of the strange, carved chairs, the wooden wing hiding half of his face, and I saw a single eye. And the eye appeared to me through glass. It was not my reading spectacles (which I had just used to inspect a new picture Giles had bought), for I removed them instantly and made as if to wipe some speck from the lens.

No, the glass was over his eye still, and then briefly, before it disappeared, the glass *was* his eye: my little crater of the linen-room window.

I couldn't for a moment tell where I was: in his house, talking informally with them or back, alone, in the little room that fits me like a shell. I had the physical sensation of imbalance and threw out one arm to steady myself. My knuckles struck against a small coffee-table that tilted and in its turn slid an onyx dish against the plaster wall.

Its impact gave out a single sharp click, like a pebble thrown against a window, or even the amplified sound of an electric switch.

At once my confusion lifted and I was clearly in company again, actually involved in speaking, with my high precise voice, of preserving dahlia tubers from the frost.

I was aware of so much then, instantly, for in that moment I recognised that to me two things had become identical—Giles' compelling eye and the small focus of my private camera upon life, the hole in the lefthand lower pane of the linen-room window. The two are intimately connected, sometimes superimposed and indistinguishable in my consciousness, for both have the same effect of spell-binding my will. Both are hypnotic.

Even as I realised this, I was on my guard. Instantly fixing my mind on other things I watched the man start up, dazed, and as I reached calmly to reset the displaced dish I hesitated, turning it deliberately in my fingers, tracing the flow of veins in its cold, smooth surface. And then I looked quickly back at Giles. He was deeply disturbed, almost desperate.

How much of my revelation he was aware of was uncertain, but he knew I had just moved apart, out of reach. And still he made efforts to recall me. It was Edward's presence that saved me, for although the habit of domination was strong between us, yet Giles dared not reveal this power openly before someone else.

I turned to Edward. "Do you remember...?" I began, and ran rapidly through a sequence of childhood recollections so rich in counterpoint emotions that it must surely baffle any other mind that attempted to break in on the unspoken communication. I saw Giles grow exhausted before my eyes, unable to penetrate such complex material. I knew that for his own safety he must give up exerting his influence for some time.

In the respite this granted I came back here to the linen-cupboard where I moved everything around. Now I write looking inwards. The window, Greenshards, all outside influences, are at my back. I still command the rooftops and the small triangle of lawn, but they are all reflected in the tilted mirror of the old dressing-table on which my papers lie. In it the window-pane's hole once more becomes central if I move aside my head, but otherwise I block it.

Giles no longer has access to my mind unless I so choose. Now, as I look up from writing, it is my own eyes I encounter. Two, set squarely in an otherwise distorted face. A strange face, somehow unfamiliar in the tilted mirror. And if he has been able to master this mind inside, why should I not do the same?

More than the furniture's position has changed; it is as though a new perspective obtains. And the new disposition has this significance, a rightness that I grow hourly more conscious of—that a deliberate decision has been made: a new control is taking over.

Before me the mirror, a framed picture. A distant landscape glimpsed through a window; nearer, the confines of a room, narrow and shadowed; in the foreground the outline of a seated woman; centrally a face, and still this is frame within frame within frame. At the heart of the picture are eyes, which, as I stare, slowly dissolve together and become one, burning darkly. Within, only sometimes showing through, is something unaccountable that waits.

I must take my time. I will not be rushed. It has taken me more than three decades to become myself, enclosed and unexamined. I cannot in a single second know what is inside this person Olive. But starting outside, as in appreciating this picture, I can travel surely towards the centre, moving back from time to time to recall the whole. Using the mirror's frame to confine my view.

Just so must she have sat to work her tapestry, the ill-fated Lady of Shalott, never looking down to where Camelot's gay flags streamed in the free wind, but seeing all that was without, at an angle in her glass. And safer so. Life at one remove, until Lancelot came up in her mirror and she ran to the window, reaching out not just to see him one fragile moment real, but to be seen herself, to feel the moving air on her hands, her cheek, be one with what lived, and have done for ever with images.

Poor accursed creature, so beautiful herself but unseen, ensnared by beauty glimpsed in a reflection. Is that me? Is my manuscript the web that 'floated wide'? Here is my mirror and in it all my little world that I have chosen, for safety, to set at one remove. If it should break, this glass, mine would do more than crack from side to side. It would shatter into a thousand fragments of my self.

And Sir Lancelot? No, the one whose image I see on the 'road that runs for ever' is Merlin himself, the timeless Magician. Lancelot is someone else again, and I know every line of his face, every movement, every sound.

At length I turned out the light and waited for morning to come over the world outside. The night was starless and very black upon the ground, the sky like a smeared reflection in old pewter curved above it. Then, for some unknown reason, I lit the candles on the dressing-table, a clay-cold ornamental pair that originally were rosy pink—some present once from Martine—but with time have faded to the tint of dead Caucasian flesh. And I sat, staring by that moving light full into the face before me. Terrible, with alien eyes looking out.

The longer I stare the more I know, and the more I am mortally afraid. And yet not I—not the I of the eyes. (Surely there is some awful significance in the sound of those words being the same?) There is an I afraid and an I that is not, that revels in its ever-growing power. An I possessed and an I possessor.

It is Olive Minton that is afraid. The other part has yet to take a name.

These are the two sums of existence, for the outside world could not exist without them. They include everything that has ever happened, every thought, every movement, every experience. Between them they remember the slightest, least-welcomed association that the persona presumes to judge upon, and even, temporarily, represses. But now I know what I am—persona and anima —with polarity, like an electric field. Persona is my negative, my restrictions, my deformity, my subservience. Persona is the unfulfilled one known as Olive

Minton. *I* am another, something finer and stronger that only now emerges, yet was always here. *I...I am Anima!*

Poor Olive Minton. I allowed her to creep back, tired and beaten, as the dawn did its tricks with the sky. She turned away from the mirror where only I can now be seen, and she put out the candles with a shudder, wanting just to get back in bed, hide her head under the blankets like a child in a thunderstorm. But from habit she is so dutiful, so submissive, poor dim shell, that she went instead to take her habitual bath and get dressed for the new day, my day. She knows what has occurred, but she has not the spirit to resist me any more. In her way she has fought me all along, but tonight was our last battle. Overcome already by love, she was the more ready to yield to me. And I have drawn the strength off her.

Tonight she has acknowledged me; she has given me my name! All her early superstitions of religion tell her I am the ultimate in herself. Without me, she knows herself to be a void—like Fenella, whom she despises. But Fenella is a persona that has never resisted, possessed by no anima. I have flowed into and out of her as steam is breathed into air and lost, and then becomes separate again, condensing on a cooler surface. I am what Giles loves when he holds Fenella in his arms, what he worships within the shell Olive. I am. Since before time was, I am.

And Olive, what of her? Between her household tasks she goes down to the garden, to Greenshards. The larches are still woody and grey-splintered. Beneath them the lacerated grass is pierced by the first stiff-spiked snow-drops. An occasional troll-like blob of white puffs from the ground between gnarled tree-roots and is a premature crocus, stillborn and wrapped in its pallid caul with the deformities of fungus, never to flower. She says goodbye all round her.

She comes patiently up to her small, narrow room under the roof and faces the window. She may look out now. Once the curse has been invoked there is nothing more to dread. Her web has floated wide: the mirror is indeed cracked from side to side, but it takes a little time for her to die. The Lady of Shalott is free now to find her boat, cast off and float downriver to Camelot. Some, when they speak of death, talk of 'taking' a life. But they are wrong. Really one 'looses' life, sets it free, casting off the husk.

Olive does not quite understand yet, but she accepts that it is so. Once more she puts her finger on the fine thread of air that enters by the hole in the shattered pane, and vaguely, not at first seeing its connection, remembers a museum in Brussels. I let her fumble with our mind, travelling back in time, supplying details where she cannot reach them, sharing again with her the long-gone sensations of adventure and being young.

Her finger feels the ridged grain of a canvas under its hard-painted veneer; she sees herself peering through her pocket magnifying glass at a hand in a portrait. Some picture by Frans Hals.

She looks close and finds, instead of a wonder of fine organic detail, that in close-up the masterpiece has melted the skin and sinews into separate tints and depths of pigment. The hand disintegrates entirely from its human form into a two-dimensional, mosaic medium.

She moves away, distressed as at some premonition, even half-sensing in her uncanny way a ghost of the two of us projected from the future into her then single mind.

From across the gallery an attendant comes up and points to the object in her hand. It is forbidden, he tells her, to use a glass to examine the pictures. Abashed as she is, she still asks why that should be. He doesn't know: he is not a man who asks himself questions, just stands there and sees that regulations are observed.

Olive is half way down the steps from the museum when she realises the answer. Strong sunlight streaming in by the gallery's roof-glass might concentrate through the lens and burn the canvas. There was real danger of damage.

A practical rule; but on that day there had been no sun. Olive went out into a grey street swept by gusty rain and laughed under her umbrella all the way across the Place Royale.

She does not laugh now. I watch her as she sits thinking how much of her life she has spent looking through glass and missing the true forms.

Now is the time to take her into my confidence. 'Olive, come here. Look at me, in the mirror. You know who I am, that you can trust me.'

She sits looking down at the hands in her lap, twisting them together so that they are like small creatures wrestling. She knows it must be soon, that I have the solution for us both, and that, having always submitted, she will do so again, finally.

'Olive, I will make you an offer. If you will hear me out quietly and agree now, I will let you come back just once more. You shall put the last word to the manuscript. Briefly. But hear me now and I will let you say goodbye.'

This is my moment. Our eyes have met in the mirror. She is mine.

Do not forget me—Olive Minton. What can I say in the time that is left me?

I recall giving birth: how it was easier to go with it, how submitting made it simple and right. With death I know it must be the same. I shall not resist her—Anima. I have little enough to lose: she has everything to gain.

Oh, Edwa--

PART TWO

MEGAN

I

Fulverton
February 6th.

MY DEAR, DEAR Sammy,

Thank you for your sweet letter. It was waiting for me when I returned from the funeral.

I don't know who said lightning never strikes the same place twice, but it's quite untrue. There must be certain exposed sites where lightning is much more likely, and there are just as surely people who've been singled out for repeated misfortunes. I feel we have had more than a normal share of disasters in these last few months. First the terrible tragedy of Martine, and now Olive snatched from us. It's frightening, as though our time for being carefree is officially past and now we must endure the reverses.

Edward maintains that neither was a sudden thing, but both had roots in the past and took their time to come about. This is the way shock takes him. As though by homespun philosophy he can make what is repugnant endurable! But then he accepts what old Hepworth said about Martine's haemorrhage; that she had this congenital weakness. As though a small blood vessel in such a healthy child could be the decisive factor of her living or not! I don't imagine he is deliberately covering up for anyone, nor that anyone in their sane mind could have intended such terrible damage to a child, but the fact remains that it is easily enough done. Other children *are* rough in their play, and undoubtedly Martine was thrown from her pony at least once during that last week when she was away. There are a hundred possibilities, and merely because they could find no obvious bruising is no excuse for dismissing the entire question of external injury. It is a much more likely thing to have happened, for she was a healthy child who had every chance of growing up strong and happy. But Hepworth is a fool, a well-meaning one no doubt, who wishes to avoid 'unpleasantness' and imagines we may find this medical mumbo-jumbo less unpalatable. But I maintain that his findings weren't a true representation of the facts, and Edward should have insisted upon a second opinion as to the cause of death. Why, Olive herself, in an impatient moment, may have pushed her so that she fell against the birdbath and damaged her head. There was no one else in the garden at the time, so we have only Olive's word for what happened. That might in some way account for much of Olive's morose strangeness in the months since. I wonder, mightn't that be partly the reason, subconscious perhaps, behind Olive's fatal crash with the car? Didn't Freud say there was no entirely unintentional accident, but always some thread of motive involved? She may have felt she needed punishment. Heaven knows, Olive, if anyone, would have repaid a Freudian analyst. She was such an inhibited, withdrawn sort of person. It always amazed me that she got on so well with the children, for they were both—Andrew still is—so open and outgoing. Perhaps the attraction of opposites. I must say, as well as being appalled by the tragic accident, we miss her dreadfully, but Edward allows it to depress him to a morbid extent.

The police have not come up with any cause for it happening. As far as they could tell from the state of the car—or of as much as wasn't completely burnt out—it was functioning normally up to that moment. I imagine it would take a little black box—as in aircraft—to be one hundred per cent sure of this, so the police may well be turning a blind eye (like Hepworth) to unpleasant possibilities. Not that that is what their function's supposed to be. I must say in some of my dealings with them, they've seemed unduly suspicious! As on that memorable night when we sat out the thunderstorm in the back of your Rover on Wimbledon Common. Darling, can you imagine the repercussions if it had happened back here in the village? The ducking-stool, anonymous phone calls, and me drummed off the hospital committee at least. How feudal we are here, and how I long to be with you again in darling, sophisticated London.

It's ridiculous how difficult it is to find someone to live here in place of Olive. The day of the dedicated spinster is gone, sad to say. Poor dear, she may not have been particularly appealing, but she had her niche. I can barely remember how it was before we had her. From the way she spoke you would have thought she'd always run Edward's house. In fact she lived here only until she was in her teens, brought up with Edward as a poor relation. But she had some kind of breakdown—in my opinion the Mintons are all more than a teeny bit dotty—and when she'd recovered, Edward's father gave her an allowance to travel on the continent.

I wish *I*'d had her chances in *my* teens. But, instead of having a wild and wonderful time and falling madly in love with some gorgeous, bearded artist of the Left Bank, she drearily returned to work for a blue-stocking degree. I think she did do pretty well at that, and then held a teaching post for a few years in Sussex. By then Edward had lost his father with a stroke and was making gentlemanly sorties to London every weekend to lay seige to a certain stage door. He must have been a much more decisive person then, but of course I was very young. Ah, '*si jeunesse savait*', indeed; though the second half of the saying is hardly appropriate, is it, my darling? Do you know, I can actually hear you laugh. That deep, merry rumble. Such a real, hair-on-chest sound.

Darling, I *long* to be with you. I shall pursue some local worthy, however unsuitable, and insist she take over the house and Edward here. Then I shall plead pressure of my career and come flying to you.

How can you bear those fusty rooms without my fallals, as you call them, lying about? And *me*.

I am with you in spirit, as no doubt the ethereal Fenella would say, were she able. She, by the way, continues in the same condition. We're not yet allowed to see her, and anyway it would do no good, for she has never opened her eyes since it happened. Yet Hepworth says she seems almost to know when anyone is with her and sometimes mumbles incoherently. I doubt the poor thing's mind will have gone entirely if she ever does wake up. It would be as well, I suppose, if she doesn't.

I keep returning to the most lugubrious subjects. It is typical of my present *tristesse*. Without you, I am a mere wraith of my former self. Do go on writing. The phone calls are lovely, but I have nothing to put under my pillow from them. Aren't I absurd? But it makes fools of us all, as you have said.

Soon, soon, soon!

Your

Megan.

February 11th.

You wicked, darling man,

Your letter was a delight, the description of your new mattress sheer poetry. I experience a *frisson* even to read of it. But how could I leave a letter like that lying about? I would have burnt it as you asked, but it burst into flames on its own. Truly! It arrived white-hot, and has blistered the E.P.N.S. of the lordly dish they bore it to me on. You are deliciously impossible and now I know what you do all those long, lonely years at sea, you salacious sailors. An imagination such as yours never came overnight and without practice!

It has done me so much good to hear from you, for on this front all is most dismal and void. My agent rang two days ago to offer a possible part with Sherman. It would have been just right, enough to keep me in town but not enough to make excessive demands on either time or energy! So right in fact that I decided to hug it to myself until it was a *fait accompli*. But now there is some wretched hangup over the money and it looks as though they can't start rehearsing until we're into the new financial year. *April*, several lifetimes away!

Nor have I been lucky over the housekeeper question.

I have dropped more than one hint in Mrs. Fenwick's hearing but to no avail. I'm sure it wouldn't overtax her to take on Edward's meals too, particularly since Giles employs her so little at present. He is still practically living at the hospital, and to go by his appearance when he last called to give a progress report, he's eating nothing at all. Edward too is as little interested in food as ever. It is really too unjust that I should be kept here, tied by no more than convention, to provide meals for a man who doesn't see me and won't eat anyway. I think Olive must have had him hooked on some secret ingredient that I've not yet come across in the larder. Do you realise I could be thinking up lovely dishes for *you*? Not that the kitchen is where I shine, for I'm no hausfrau, thank God. But there are other accomplishments, and there ... Agreed?

You asked about the saga of Olive. I hadn't realised you were so taken with my late cousin-in-law. Well, it was when Andrew was a baby that she started visiting us. She had just given up her teaching—another breakdown of sorts, for she was quite unstable; depressive I suppose you would call it. Her father committed suicide when she was eleven or twelve, and I suppose it aroused a morbid strain in her.

I've thought quite often since she died that she may have meant it to happen. Suicide does, I believe, run in families. Of course, having Fenella in the car with her at the time makes that seem less likely, but if she'd been wholly sane she wouldn't have thought of it anyway. How can we know how it takes them at the last? Now that I look back, I see she was working up to a crisis of some kind. She must have been a little mad, in a harmless way, for quite a while. Then the shock of Martine's death, (whether or not she held herself responsible for it,) coupled with the unfortunate influence of the Blanchards over the past year, seems quite to have unhinged her. We were lucky she didn't pick on some more damaging means of doing away with herself. Why, she might have done a Lizzie Borden all round, or set the house on fire. It makes the blood run cold to think of it.

However, back to the life history: I had had more than my fill of sterilising feeding bottles and airing nappies when there was an offer of a part in a touring company of *Oklahoma*. The original girl who 'cain't say no'; no less. Family finances were a little low and Edward was worried about putting Andrew down for his old school. Olive stepped in with the offer to hold the fort until I could get back. When eventually I did, she'd settled in and was very busy making herself indispensable. You've heard of in-laws who come to tea and stay ten years? Olive was with us twelve. Of course, the arrangement had its advantages, for she shared a lot of Edward's fuddy-duddy interests and didn't mind all the messy part of coping with children. Why, when Martine was born I barely saw the baby for the first few months. I had a pretty bad time of it and Edward suggested a winter in Malta with friends who had taken a house there. Just think, you might have called there yourself, resplendent in gold braid, in one of those intervals between splicing mainbraces and manning the bridge club. But I would certainly have remembered you if you had. There were some delightful young officers came

ashore, but you weren't one of them. If you had been—
who knows? Perhaps we should not be apart as we are
now, for at that time I'd almost made up my mind to
leave Edward, or rather, not to come back here. However, I did, and have done my dutiful best for him over
the years ever since.

What abysmal waste; for what has he made of it and
of me? I am a prisoner, a domestic tame thing, second-
class-citizen-type woman. Sammy, we must evolve some
way of being together. For all you say in your sizzling
missives, I think you are too patient.

Burn, burn, burn!

—until I am with you again.

Your

Megan.

Fulverton,
Eve of St. Valentine's Day!

My Darling,

I should be sadly neglecting my religious duties (and
raised a Welsh Baptist, at that!) if I didn't celebrate the
Saint's Day with a little valentine of my own. To write
is such a very poor substitute for being with you—in
which delectable case you can surely imagine what I
should feel compelled to do about it—that I am wringing
my hands to know how best to convey my feelings. Words
are out, as being utterly improper, if spades are to be
called spades. (Darling, has it struck you how the
language of love is based on the card suits? Hearts,
diamonds, spades, clubs—or even clubs before spades, in
the *crime passionel*!: a wry summary of the disintegrat-

ing affaire.) After that cynical digression I shall confine my ardour to breathing hotly on the paper and allow psychic vibrations to convey this intimately to you.

Which of course brings Fenella the Fey to mind. There has been some slight improvement in her condition. That is, she neither moves nor speaks, but her eyes are sometimes open. As I expected, the poor creature's mind seems completely to have gone now. The doctors talk a great deal of specious rubbish, but her neurologist (the London man who's always had a finger on her pulse, so to speak) is flummoxed. They mention aboulia, anoesis and something else equally Greek, but what they mean, I think, is that she can't (and/or won't) cope with reality. Well, frankly, was it ever her strong point? She and Olive were a pair. Oh, I know you admire F but you must admit it's more for her physical charms than her native wit. And your insistence that Giles is such a 'decent fellow'! Decent is hardly the word that would slip into my mind to describe him. Strange, *sinister* even; that's more like it. I've always found him—not disturbing, which is familiar and rather pleasant, but—*eerie*. Yes, that's it absolutely.

He's in a terrible state over Fenella, watching her like a hawk a rabbit. It's hardly surprising that she isn't forthcoming. One can't help wondering if all this concern isn't just a little overdone. Suppose, for example, it's really a cover for some other emotion—despair that she didn't actually get killed? Or fear of what she may reveal if ever she does again speak or write? He is so perfectly cast for a villain, you see. The actress in me can't bear to waste a good part!

You asked after Edward. What touching concern! He is as always. What more damning thing could I say? His latest dreary complaint against me is that I allow sparrows to eat the crocus heads. Apparently Olive used to devote hours to winding cotton thread among twigs to keep the birds off. Well, 'big deal', as Andrew would say. It makes me feel so impatient, so restricted, to be limited to his tiny world. What is a wasted crocus compared to me?

Need I be wasted, though? I agree it is a little early for you to be coming here, in view of the family mourning and such, and entertaining is still awkward as there's no one yet to take over Olive's job, but we could meet somewhere half way. Do set yourself to mastermind something really lovely that we shall remember always. Then I will do my share in devising a reason to be away from home. It could do a lot for you, my sweet.

Till then I droop, I do really.

Your

Megan.

Fulverton,
February 21st.

Sammy, my sweet,

I hope you are noting that over a whole week has elapsed since I last wrote—and this to mark that I'm not entirely gruntled. (Isn't that a gorgeous word? I always think of little, pink piglets snuggled on fresh straw—though at near-hand they faintly disgust me!) But truly, darling, aren't you being just the tiniest bit awkward? I know the Admiralty revolves about you, the sea lords are demanding and the social pressures in London at present are more than a career bachelor such as yourself can resist, *but* ... Well, I shall say no more. But when Whitehall in its wisdom sends the relief party ashore to go a-mermaiding, I trust you to be of the party. A captain surely gets only one chance to stay and go down with his ship! And yes, that *is* almost a threat.

There is little here to be gay about, but thank you for your rather prim little appreciation of my last letter. I do my best, sir, for all my gentlemen. (Bobs curtsey and exits left pertly. Re-enters centre back bravely smiling and in Pagliacci costume.)

You are right that we don't appear to share each other's opinions on the Blanchards, and I have been wondering just when this devotion of yours to them really began. Until the evening you met them here you were quite prepared to suspect them of more than a slight case of skulduggery. Yet almost as soon as you laid eyes on them there was suddenly no more deserving couple for your plaudits. They appeared to me absolutely ordinary on that occasion, even perhaps a little wooden, but you were evidently enchanted. Nevertheless it doesn't give you the right to criticise me so sharply when I discover anything mildly suspicious in the behaviour of either one. And Giles has been decidedly odd of late, whatever you may have thought of his earlier attitudes. Sammy, if I can't write to you about my uneasiness, who can I tell? Edward is so preoccupied with his own miseries that he has no ears for me. But something very strange is going on and Giles Blanchard is at its centre. Do you know that yesterday I actually discovered him creeping about *inside this house*? Let me tell you what happened.

I'd forgotten it was laundry day and hadn't humped the box down from the linen-room till Mrs. Benson reminded me mid-afternoon. Normally I take a snooze with a magazine about this time, but as Mrs. B 'has a back' (such as no self-respecting domestic can afford not to use against her long-suffering employer) there was nothing for it but to run up there and then. And there was Milord Blanchard half way through the contents of the linen press. And what do you think his excuse was? For being there, uninvited, inside my house—that he hadn't wished to disturb my rest-hour. For stacking a great pile of laundered linen in the middle of the bare wooden floor—that he was looking for something Olive had promised to drop across!

Now you know as well as I do that the Blanchards are in no need of our cast-off, sides-to-middle, Olive-mended sheets. I didn't have to do more than raise my eyebrows, but I did it rather thoroughly. For a moment the imperturbable Giles was completely off balance. Then he explained that she had been writing a diary of sorts. It had been on his suggestion, and he had promised to look it through to see if it was worth her trying to get it published. A sort of half-fictional, half-autobiographical country journal. She'd been at it for two or three months, he said, and was very diffident about anyone's being allowed to see it. She had told him she wrote it up in this room in her spare moments and kept it hidden under the highest pile of linen. He even had the audacity to suggest I should help him to go through the remainder of the cupboard!

What an absolutely idiotic thing to make up! I would have given him credit for more imagination than that, though of course he was taken completely off guard and hadn't time for elaborate invention.

I just laughed and said Olive must have been teasing him (and can you imagine *that*?) for she would never have dreamed of disturbing a sacrosanct pile of clean linen. With her it amounted to *lèse-majesté* at least.

Darling, you should have seen him. *He blazed.* I had never appreciated my husband's cousin: she had a sensitivity and a fine balance of mind that was quite out of the ordinary. And on and on. But one very curious thing that struck me immediately about him: he spoke all the time in the present, as though she were still alive. I do honestly believe he must have forgotten she was dead. That is how much he cares for poor Olive and her fictitious manuscript.

But what can he have been up to, do you think? He hadn't just dived in there to be out of the way when he heard me coming, because there wouldn't have been time to dislodge all that linen—several armfuls. And besides I had kicked off my shoes downstairs and the landing carpet deadened my steps.

I'm convinced there was something he expected to find in that cupboard. But not a diary surely! If I had the energy I'd clear everything out and look. Perhaps I can persuade Mrs. Benson to list what we've got in there. Wouldn't it be a hoot if Olive had really been keeping a journal? Perhaps it would say what she thought of me. And did that frigid virgin fall, I ask myself, for the handsome lieutenant-commander?

But anyway you'll agree now that Giles' behaviour is more than a little fishy. I consider it, even for a Blanchard, distinctly odd. Again I find myself wondering what sinister thing he is covering up this time. You remember I told you how Fenella had been drugging. Oh, legitimately, I grant you, because the neurologist had prescribed the capsules. Suppose—just *suppose*—that Olive had some pills too, ones that Giles had slipped out of Fenella's supply. What effect would they have had on someone they weren't prescribed for? And don't forget that Giles was a qualified doctor, or so he claims. I believe I'm on to something there! I must work this out and write again when I see how it all fits together. You never would believe me when I raised the question of his first wife, the real Fenella. But this *can't* be the same one, Sammy. I'm sure if you think it over again and give consideration to the dates, you'll see she can't have looked 'exactly the same' the second time you met her. After nearly twenty years? I wish you had an old photograph of her to check by. Sammy, don't you see how terribly important, and dangerous, this is? This could have been his second attempt to kill. And if he did engineer the crash, he was prepared to destroy Olive too, an innocent bystander. If he will risk that, there are no limits he won't go to. I am scared, Sammy. Perhaps I should try to tell Edward, but he's in another world. And then he's so deadly legalistic he would tie all my reasoning up. But I *know* I'm right. With people I don't have to work things out to prove anything. I know Giles is evil. I've always known he's evil. The only thing I'm not sure of is exactly what he's done.

Sammy darling, do think back clearly. Forget this girl you met here with Giles. Think; what was the first Fenella like? And *please* don't be so absurdly rigid about this one subject of Giles Blanchard. Isn't there the least possibility that he might be less than perfect?

Which by now I am afraid you'll rather think—

Your

Megan.

2

Fulverton,
Sunday.

SAMMY, DARLING,

I cannot wait for your reply to my last letter before sending you word that now I have been *proved* right.

Giles phoned last night to say that Hepworth had suggested we visit Fenella in hospital. She is physically so much improved but her mind trails behind, as I think I have already told you. It was the doctors' idea that if she saw some friends from the neighbourhood it might stimulate her to come alive. They put it more technically, but that is what they meant. Apparently Hepworth had made this suggestion last week but Giles didn't take it up. He still wasn't keen when he came to drive us down, Edward and me, this afternoon. I had some qualms about being in the same car with him, but he could hardly do us any harm while we were all together. We went in his new, dark red Bentley that has replaced the smashed Mercedes. Very comfortable, but still terrifying.

I don't know how to describe the change we found in Fenella. She looks so well. You remember what a droopy creature she used to be? She lay there with her black hair wild all over the pillow and her eyes absolutely ablaze. They had intended to cut her hair short, Sister said, but she had some kind of convulsion and they gave up.

I was quite wrong about the state of her mind; it is there all right and functioning, but she doesn't seem able to move or speak. It must be terribly frustrating. You could sense as you went in that she was furious at being so powerless.

We unloaded the grapes and peaches and mumbled on about things in general. I invented some messages of goodwill from Andrew and yourself. I realised then that I'd no idea whether she knew Olive was dead. It made me go hot and cold, because if not she'd surely be expecting a message from her. However, I skipped on to something else. In a way it was a typical conversation with Fenella: she's never been exactly responsive. Only now there was this difference, that although she made no sound and never moved so much as a finger she made you so conscious of her. Do you know what I mean?

All the time we were there Giles stayed close and I had no chance to whisper. I had given a lot of thought to what I should say. I tried to imagine what it would be like to lie there, helpless, unable to communicate, while the man who had tried to murder her stood guard between her and anyone who might otherwise be made to understand the danger. I felt myself lying there like that and Giles waiting to silence my very first word. I was determined that somehow I would get to see her on my own. And then suddenly the chance came. The neurologist was just leaving for London and wanted a word first with Giles.

We were in a private ward but the Sister stayed with us. I felt her very cagily watching as I went up to the bed and touched Fenella's hand. (I am still calling her Fenella, though it's certainly not her name.)

I bent over her and whispered, *"Who are you? Who?"*

The effect was magical. Her face quivered. It was joy, I'm sure, because someone had guessed and she wasn't cut off any more. The Sister came rustling up and tried to make me stand back, but the girl's mouth was moving. We all crowded round her. Sister had her hand out ready to press the bell.

And then she spoke, in a funny dried-up sort of voice, as though she wasn't used to speaking. "A-A-Ann," she said, And then again, more confidently, "Ann. Ann. I am Anne-Ma..."

She stopped there, mouth still open, and looked past us to the door. Giles had just come silently in and was staring at her. He looked like Lucifer, beautiful and unspeakably evil. Sammy, I have never been so scared in all my life.

Darling, do something for me, please. You are the only one who remembers what happened all those years ago. Can you somehow find out her name, the young *au pair* girl who was supposed to have been burnt to death? The local papers must have carried the story: If only you can get the right date, one long-distance phone call would settle it. Do that, *please*. I know we shall hear she was called Anne-Marie, perhaps a German or Swiss girl. You see, my intuition was right all along. Perhaps now you will be sorry you defended Giles against my judgment. He's not worth it. The man is a monster.

Phone me as soon as you have confirmation of the name. I shan't tell Edward until I have that proof.

In great haste and as ever with all my love, darling,
Your
Megan.

Fulverton,
February 26th.

Sammy, dear,

You must have thought my behaviour when you phoned last night utterly barbarous. I do hope you will forgive it when you know the full circumstances. As I just had time to say then, we are very much alarmed about Edward. As you know, ever since Olive's accident he has kept himself apart, in a sort of deep melancholia. I had hoped that with time he would find some interest in less morbid topics, as he did after Martine died. However the effects seem to have been accumulative and now he has completely collapsed.

It happened Sunday night, after I had written to you. When I slipped back from posting your letter, I saw the light still on in his study and thought I'd take him some coffee in. Lately he has started this habit of keeping a full decanter in there for company and when he drags himself to bed it sounds as though he's been working solidly through it. However it's always full again in the morning so I assume he tops it up from bottles kept locked in the desk. I don't care at all for it because that was really the ruin of his uncle, Olive's father, and you know how he ended!

So, to offer an alternative (and to see for myself how far his 'work' had progressed) I took in the coffee. I found him collapsed over the desk in a dark pool that I took at first for blood but then realised was ink. He'd been in the act of filling his pen when he had some kind of fit. His face was a terrible colour and he was breathing oddly. I panicked, thought he'd taken poison or something and rang straight through to the hospital. There wasn't an ambulance manned at the time but Frobisher, the House Physician, was there and came up himself. We loaded Edward into his car and I went down to stay near his bedside all night.

I can't tell you how awful it was. It was Martine all over again. As the clock hands came round towards two I was sure they were going to come and tell me he had gone. Sammy, I felt guilty as hell. Can you understand that?

I must have fallen asleep at last—sometime after four —still waiting to hear the worst. The minute I woke I remembered, and thought that if only I'd stayed awake and concentrated hard maybe I could have stopped him slipping away. But he hadn't gone. A nurse brought me tea and was quite casual. She said Edward had been sleeping normally for over an hour. She suggested that if I went home then and came back about eleven, after the doctors had done their rounds, I could see him. I wanted to slap the little cat's face!

It wasn't poison, of course, nor a coronary, but a violent shock reaction. These Minton sensibilities! The doctors cross-examined me about what exactly he'd been up to all the day before. Well, apart from visiting Fe— the Blanchard girl—with me, I couldn't say for sure. He'd been in the study with his legal papers. Maybe something in them upset him. Of course, he did hear the girl say her real name, but I doubt if he would see the significance of this because, since that early occasion before you first came here, I've never mentioned my suspicions to him. As like as not he thought she was merely confused.

You would think, wouldn't you, after a collapse like that he'd be different? Shocked into gratitude for not having died, or something. But Edward wasn't. He is just the same as before; quiet and grey and anxious. His first concern was for the documents he'd left out on the desk. What had I done with them and so on. I told him I'd just got Mrs. Benson to run the wet ink off and bundle them into a drawer. They'd be there for when he came home.

And then there was nothing for it but he wanted to come home straight away, so old Hepworth said I'd better stay on at the hospital myself and help to keep his mind at rest. Which I dutifully did, and it was during a quick trip back to the house for some magazines Monday evening that I took your phone call. I was still rather anxious about Edward and afraid he might try to get up while I was away. I truly didn't mean to snap at you, sweet. I was frightened, that's all.

You started to say something about Giles and the fire that killed his wife. Have you found out the girl's full name? There's not such a rush to have it now because I wouldn't dare to worry Edward yet awhile with anything fresh. Even if I go to the local police he would be involved in the backwash, so I must be patient and make no move for the present. But I am eager to hear what you have managed to find out. I tried twice in the last day to see the girl on my own, but Giles is always there. The nurses think that he dotes on his wife, but it makes me quite shudder. Poor creature, suppose she really did get the chance to tell me the truth about herself. What do you think he would do if he found out—to her and to me? Really I shall have to manage it most carefully, with a witness present, shan't I? It's no use depending on the nurses here; they're all besotted with the man. There was a policeman sitting by her bedside for the first two days after the accident, but when it became apparent that she was paralysed (or whatever) he was withdrawn. Now they seem to be waiting for her to regain her speech properly before she makes a deposition. By then Giles will have her suitably schooled in his version, I'm sure. It's so unfair, and so dangerous, this power he has to make everybody believe him and do just as he wants. Remember how you fell yourself for his personal magnetism. And you with all that man-management experience! I think I shall even mistrust myself a little whenever anyone says I'm 'charming' again.

Do please ring me tomorrow, at home after seven. I promise it won't be a 'hot line' this time—or not in the same sense. I look forward to hearing your manly voice.

A bientôt, chéri,

Megan.

Fulverton
March 1st.

My dear, distant Sammy,

Your brief note telling of the Gibraltar trip crossed, I think, with my letter explaining about Edward's collapse.

I do hope it has caught up with you by now and is not lingering somewhere in your flat awaiting your return.

I am appalled by the suddenness of your departure, especially as I thought you had passed into some department less intimately connected with ships than with the ducks in St. James's Park.

I shall assume that you are *au fait* with matters here and continue the saga from where I left it at last time of writing. The main item concerns Edward. He is home again and functioning much as before his attack. If anything I should say he seems more preoccupied and somehow shrunken. I have made several real attempts to get him talking normally and taking an interest in things about him, but it is quite useless. He will follow me for a little while and smile patiently, but gradually he drifts off into a world of his own. I think the drinking must have been going on secretly much longer than I had suspected.

Galbraith was up here from the office with some papers and I sounded him out about matters inside the firm. He was inclined to hedge at first but when he saw I was determined to have the truth he came out with it. They have all been very uneasy about Edward for some time, but particularly over the last fortnight before his illness. He has been so forgetful and has even cancelled appointments with clients without offering any excuse. I tried to find out whether he had any financial worries, but Galbraith became very stuffy at that and said that if I wished to have accountants called in I should approach Edward's partners, not himself. Just in case that was meant as an oblique hint, I shall go one better and get

on to their wives. Each separately, of course. I'm going
to drive Clara Minns into Salisbury tomorrow and Jo
Carpenter is lunching with me at Dorlands' next day.

It is a bleak, blustery day here and Spring seems a long
way off. I shall have to work myself into some sort of
enthusiasm for Andrew's coming home, which is in less
than four weeks now. It seems he is no sooner back at
school than they turn him round and send him home
again. Ideally we should all go away somewhere cheerful
and warm. Majorca would be pleasant. And maybe near
enough for you to slip across and see us? I shall put it to
Edward, but frankly I doubt if he has the energy to face
the idea of travelling.

Do you know where I found him last night? I'd gone
into the study, just to see how things were (how the
decanter stood!) and found the room empty, with the
french windows unlocked and one curtain pulled open.
It was chilly, with a flurry of sleet in the wind now and
then but he'd gone out, through the garden without coat
or macintosh. Nothing for it but to follow, so I snatched
some clothes up and ran out after him. I must have been
searching for over ten minutes, calling and flashing my
torch, when he stepped out of the gap in the beech hedge
between Greenshards' garden and our own. He must have
heard me but he had never made a sign. He said he'd
'just been looking at the house' (Greenshards), and 'had
a lot to think about'. It really is galling that when I am
making such an effort to help him he should decide to be
so unaware of me. It is as though nothing exists for him
but his secret sorrows, and it gets me more than a little
out of patience.

I have been unable to go any further with the Anne-Marie business. Giles continues to sit guard over her at the hospital, but I understand she is to be allowed home in a few days. She is talking, eating and even getting up for a few hours each day, but the longer Giles has alone with her the less chance I feel I have of ever getting her to come out into the open. He will have persuaded her that she's already too deeply involved to be considered an innocent party, and if ever they've been through a legal form of marriage she's not compelled to give evidence against him on a criminal charge, I believe. I wish I could talk to Edward about this but it's hopeless. The only chance seems to be that if I leave it a little longer and his abstraction increases he may not care one way or the other what I am stirring up. I wonder if he has considered retiring from the practice. Certainly he doesn't feel involved in it any more.

Sammy, love, I am sending this c/o the Admiralty, as your new address hasn't yet reached me. The Service, in its mysterious way (like God's), will no doubt get it to you in the end.

My love, of course, to the Apes. Do please hurry and finish whatever you have to do at Gib and come back soon to—

Your desolate
Megan.

P.S. It's a terribly long time since I last had a letter from you. Feb 16th was the last, I see, and that spiked with umbrage at my casting some slur on the revered Giles Blanchard. Sammy, you can't possibly *still* have such a good opinion of him. Surely you can't disregard all I've found out about him since then? Do write back straight away, darling, when you get this—a nice, *comfortable* letter so that I know everything's still cosy between us. Do you realise you had me worried for a moment? Silly me, M.

3

MY DEAR ANDREW,

I have taken over Daddy's little job of the weekly letter as he is really none too well at present. In fact he's had a couple of days in the cottage hospital since last weekend, but not to worry, sweet. A touch of flu, I think, and you know how he will stick at his work so. It is probably a disguised blessing in the long run as it has forced him to take things a little more easily. The weather's wretched, of course, which doesn't help, and he's been feeling rather down since Aunt Olive's funeral a month ago.

It was very considerate of you to think of asking leave to come home, but she wouldn't have expected it, you know. It's not as though she was a close relative. You are not the only one who doesn't understand how it happened. We are equally puzzled. But there again I suppose the weather had a hand in it. There may well have been a patch of black ice that was overlooked, and gone by the time anyone examined the route carefully. No, it wasn't Daddy's car but the Blanchards' Mercedes. Olive had driven it before, but what with it being dark, and the awkward business of her boot, I suppose somehow she muffed the unfamiliar controls. It just happened to be at that corner where the combe drops sheer away. It's a miracle they weren't both killed, but Mrs. Blanchard was thrown clear. Strange to say, she wasn't wearing her seat belt that night, but Olive was strapped in and didn't stand a chance. I had hoped not to go into all these details, but since you asked, there they are. Please don't refer to it all when writing back because Daddy will be seeing the letter and we must try to avoid depressing him.

These accidents are very hard to accept, especially when so many little chances bring about the circumstances. There were so many that contributed in this case —Olive's deformity and the weather and the route and the seat belt, the strange car, and Giles having phoned Fenella just when he did.

He'd been up to London for a couple of days and returned unexpectedly. When he reached the station the one-and-only taxi was off on a long trip. He tried to phone Fenella but the line was out of order, so naturally he put a call through to us and Olive took it. She offered to go across to Greenshards and warn Fenella to drive down for Giles. As it happened Fenella was about to go to bed for an early night and had taken her sleeping tablets. Actually the hospital found she must have taken a very large dose, so it's not surprising Olive offered to take over the driving. We wouldn't have known about all this but Olive stopped the car here on the way down to explain she'd be gone for half an hour. And, as you know now, she never came back.

Mrs. Blanchard cannot even remember anything that happened while Giles was away in London, let alone the fatal drive, but that's often the case with concussion. She has been suffering since, what, I think, is called hysterical paralysis—unable to move or talk, through shock. However, for the last week she's been improving slowly and now speaks, though rather haltingly like someone who has had a stammering cure and needs to concentrate on every syllable separately. And yesterday she came back to Greenshards. From the upstairs landing window I saw them drive up and Giles help her out of their new red Bentley. She is quite twisted still and hobbles with a stick. I had a terrible feeling, seeing her then all wrapped up and crooked, that it wasn't her at all but your Aunt Olive come back from the dead. And there is nothing wrong with her limbs at all, physically. She merely *thinks* that she cannot stand or walk properly. As though she has somehow taken over Olive's deformity. There, you see how lugubrious I have become! It's a ridiculous idea, isn't it?

You remember that rather nice naval man who has been here to stay twice? We heard this week that he's suddenly been sent out to Gibraltar. He's very keen that Daddy, you and I should spend part of the Easter hols out there near him. I really think it wouldn't be such a bad idea at that. Majorca can be simply gorgeous in the Spring and that would do Daddy such a lot of good, with sunshine and relaxation and a change of diet. Don't you agree? Of course, he thinks I fuss him, but if *you* were to suggest it, out of the blue, he might well agree to go. How about it, sweetie? I think we all deserve a cheerful interlude by now.

Are you getting excited about breaking up? I shudder to look out at the sleet and rain and imagine you chugging about on the rugger field in those wretched little cotton shorts and shirt. Well, next term it will be cricket or tennis, thank goodness. I believe I have a brochure somewhere of a hotel at Palma with super sand foreshore and hard tennis courts. I will look it out for you.

Do write soon, and sweetie, try to make it nice and bright for poor old Daddy, won't you?

All my love,

M.

P.S. I have just heard that old Mrs. Mullins, Mr. Blackstock's housekeeper, has pneumonia and Dr. Hepworth has arranged for a nurse to go in and look after her and the old chap. I thought you might like to drop them a line, as I know you always used to call in there with Aunt Olive.

Home,
March 10th.

My dear Andrew,

What an angry little letter! I can't imagine why you should take exception in that way to my suggestion about the Med for Easter. Perhaps you don't quite realise how hard Daddy has been working of late and how badly he needs a change. However, I appreciate I shall get no help from you in this direction, so please forget I asked you. You are perfectly right that Daddy could suggest it himself—if he were normally healthy and vigorous. Unfortunately, when you are so run-down the effort of planning is greater than the effort it requires to get anywhere, and that is why I felt we should all lean a little towards the idea and so carry him with us. It was certainly with no intention of under-handedness as you imply. I really do think, Andrew, you should consider your words before writing. I have been quite hurt by the tone of some of your remarks.

I imagine the only real reason for your writing at all this week was to enquire about that dog of Olive's. Yes, it did go to Mrs. Mullins, though I can't imagine it's much of a life for the poor creature, especially now that there's no one to take it walks or see that it's in before dark. I think it must be that one that comes howling round here of a night. I heard one barking and throwing itself against the door when Giles Blanchard was on the phone last night. It sounded as though the thing was frantic and trying to get into their house. They have never had a dog of their own because Fenella can't stand them. I imagine a black cat would be more in her line, with all the crystal-gazing and so on.

She makes steady progress, I understand. I've seen her hobbling about the garden once or twice and peering at the bulbs coming through. This is quite a new interest for her. She never had time for the garden before, except to lie in a Bahama lounger under the trees. But since the accident shook her up she appears more lively in every way, for all the difficulty she seems to have in getting about. However, with practice, she is gradually over-coming even that. Giles has been talking of a long holiday abroad, but I don't think they've settled on any particular place yet.

Bevis, at the Tennis Club, was in Daddy's office the other day when I called. He wants to know whether you wish him to book any private coaching for the holidays. I told him you were keen on organising your own time so I couldn't speak for you. Do write to him if you intend to have some lessons. Apparently he's booked a pro who's very good—and no doubt expensive—so the committee want to be sure he's made the most use of.

That seems to be all the news. Still no hope of getting a replacement in the house. We are to go to the Blanchards' on Tuesday evening for dinner, if Daddy feels up to it, so I'll be able to tell you more about Fenella's progress after that.

I do hope that by now you have recovered from your fit of spleen, or whatever, and that it didn't signal the onset of an infectious illness. You used always to be such a little horror as a small boy when you were going down with some childish complaint!

Take care of yourself, dear.

Your loving,

Mother.

P.S. I have sent Mr. Matthews a cheque for £5 in case your pocket money was getting low. Now you can wind up the term with a little celebration.

Fulverton,
March 10th.

My dear Sammy,

You have apparently vanished off the face of the earth, leaving no trace. I had quite a little trouble to ascertain from the Admiralty that your post had been redirected to you, but they were hardly forthcoming about your whereabouts. Can it be that the silent Service has rather overdone it this time and neglected to tell Whitehall just where you are? What a business all this hush-hush attitude is; it should have gone out with the war.

However, sweetie, after a silence of my own that lasted a fortnight, I am launching another missive in the hope that it will home on to you at last, and then you will know that your letters have not been reaching me. What a clutch of them there will be when they do materialise.

It is suddenly imperative that I should have that information about Anne-Marie. As I suspected, Giles' dominance has had the effect of making her clam up completely on the subject. In fact, so confident is he that she can be relied on to hold her tongue, that he doesn't bother any more chaperoning her when I call. We are free to sit and exchange feminine confidences to our heart's content, the only barrier to discovering what I wish to know being Anne-Marie herself.

I wish I could properly explain the difference in her. It is as though for the very first time I see her really well. All the earlier hesitance and nervousness is gone. She is full of confidence and vitality, as though that awful empty vapidity of hers has unaccountably filled up. Whatever he has done, or he and the accident between them, it has produced a new woman. I am convinced she is so delighted with her life as it now is, that she will never truly admit to anything that could endanger it in any way.

So you see, I must attack the problem from another angle. When Andrew gets back from school I shall have to take him around quite a bit, since we've decided against a holiday abroad, in view of Edward's poor health. I intend to spend a few days down at Plymouth with him, and then I shall be able to look up the story for myself.

If you could let me have the date, roughly, of the fire at the Blanchards' it would save me hours of scrabbling through old newspapers in the reading-room. Of course, ideally you would be back in Pompey or Portland yourself and we would have a magnificent reunion, but I suppose that is in the realm of utter fantasy? Yet I hope this difficulty in tracing you may be due to your already being on the way home. If so, you must come down here at the very first opportunity. When we have time to look at any one else I will take you to see Anne-Marie. You will certainly have something interesting to say about her transformation.

We were there last night for dinner, in the nature of a celebration. What a show they put on for us! Mrs. Fenwick must have been at it for days, and she said 'Fenella' herself had had a hand in it too. Superb *vol-au-vent*. I've never tasted any so good since Olive's. Then *escalopes de veau* followed by peaches in brandy. Choice of Edward's favourite cheeses and wines, so Giles too was evidently going out of his way to heal any breach there might be between our two houses. He was the perfect host. Now I look back on it, I recognise it was like the first dinner party given by a pair of newly-weds, but with everything going right! Yes, that is exactly how it was. And yet *we* were the ones who were nervous. Edward was at his imbecile worst and couldn't take his eyes off Fenella. (I have to call her that, or there would be a terrible lot of explaining to do if the other name slipped out! Perhaps it's as well that Giles thinks my suspicions are allayed. I am more than a little afraid of him, even though now he appears so relaxed and normal.)

I was amazed to find that they have adopted a dog! We shall have our Svengali, Giles, becoming a pipe-and-slippers man yet! Actually it is the little dachshund Edward gave Olive. I think she found it too dependent, for the poor thing doted on her. Anyway, she got rid of it to an old woman in the village who died last week. It was allowed to run wild while the old lady was ill and it took to coming to Greenshards and howling to be let in. It says a lot for Fenella's improved spirits that she's let the dog adopt her completely, for she's always hated the things.

Another thing that I'm sure will surprise you. Can you imagine Olive ever writing a book? Yet that, apparently, is what she was doing shortly before she died. And that must be what Giles referred to when he was looking in the linen cupboard. There really *is* a manuscript. Do you remember Edward spilling ink over some documents when he collapsed? We put them away in his desk without noticing what they were, except that the pages were hand-written. I automatically took it for his writing, which isn't unlike Olive's. I came across them again today when I was looking for the stapler to fix some receipts together, and when I skimmed through the top sheet I realised what it was. A sort of diary, as Giles said. Of course, his not having lied about this doesn't excuse him for sneaking into the house without my knowledge, but I admit I now feel less angry with him over the intrusion. I wonder why he was so anxious to get his hands on it without telling me? He must be afraid there's something damning about him in it, or some hurtful home truth about Fenella. Well, I shall have my chance to find out tonight, for Edward will be dining with an old client who's making a new will, so I shall have the whole evening free for going through it. Next time I write I will let you know how I find this new gem of Eng. Lit.!

Well darling, I hope this finds you and finds you well. And less distant.

Till we meet again,
As ever,
Megan.

4

IT IS INCREDIBLE! First this horrible, mad document of Olive's and now all my recent letters to Sammy returned with the curtest little cover note any pompous fool could put his name to. What a wretched, self-opinionated blimp of a man! It is abnormal, *unhealthy*, to remain so obstinate in his defence of anyone when the proof is so overwhelming. Why cannot he see?

And now there is no one to write to, for Andrew's too young by far—however mature he considers himself when censuring his mother's friendships! Oh God, who can I turn to? I'm reduced to writing to myself, like poor, mad Olive.

What did she think she was up to? How could she let herself be fooled in that way—she who had such a high opinion of her own intelligence. She was besotted with him. No, *bewitched*. Under a spell, like the Lady of Shalott she wrote of, patching sheets and weaving fantasies, seeing herself working at a tapestry that showed all humanity. 'All Human Life is Here!'—like the *News of the World* ad.—yes, my God, just like that. Staring into mirrors, doing tricks with glass—the green shards of the seance, the window with its obsessive hole, the lens she imagined over Giles' single eye—all that Kafka-Caligari nonsense. Working herself over the edge, into madness, and solemnly writing it all down step by bloody

step. And appearing so normal all the time, so contempt-
ibly *ordinary*!

It's not surprising that Edward found her testament
too much. All this weight of evidence that adds up to
only one thing—madness. Hers, her father's, her child's.

But Olive, with a *child*? It can't have been. That must
be the point where reality got right away. And yet, was
there any one point it happened at? Isn't it mad, in a
greater or less degree, all the way through? Even on the
first page, what I first took for literary pretensions, something uneven, plain odd, about the way the words go
together.

Could Edward have given her a child? When they
were—what, she fifteen and he eighteen, in his first year
at Cambridge? That was when she had her 'breakdown'.
Edward's father sent her away, paid for her to ... Oh,
my God, *my God*!

There is nothing for it, I shall have to go through it all
again, bit by bit, try and think about each little detail
one at a time. At present my mind is like a sunburst,
with thoughts, like pains, sticking out at all angles. And
none of them leading anywhere. Just starting and stop-
ping. Oh, I must think. Think. Olive tried to think it
out, and see where it took her. Only, she was mad. Funny,
I've said so often to myself, (wrote it to Sammy even)
that the Mintons are all unhinged. Well, they are. Were.
There's only Edward left now. And poor little Andrew.
You can't count that other child. Noel.

No, it couldn't be true. She imagined it all. But what
started her off? That room, and Martine coming in to
say we'd run into the Blanchards at the station. New

people next-door. Greenshards being part of Olive; its connection with her father's suicide....

All that much is true. I know it happened. What of the rest? Only Edward knows, and I can't go to him. I can't admit I've read this. I can't ask him; did you this, that? Your crippled cousin by night, in the garden, when she was only fifteen?

And yet he'll know I know. Like Bluebeard's wife I can't help giving myself away. He can't help seeing. Nothing will ever be the same again. *She* said that, when the Blanchards came. Their fault.

Giles Blanchard, see what you've done to us!

So, Edward knows.

I am not like Olive. I can't sit and cry silently inside. I must fight, and not shadows but something tangible.

Sleep was impossible. I went up to that wretched room where it all happened. There was a half-moon shining through the window. I swore as I've never sworn before and I put my fist straight through the glass and stood there screaming while the warm blood ran to my elbow and plopped about me on the floor. I didn't have to tell him I had read the thing. But I showed him, the hole isn't there any more, the little cratered hole she peered through and saw all life warped and distorted.

Now Edward can tell me it isn't true, any of it. She was mad and a poor distraught ghost and I have exorcised her. She can never come back now. Only the wind blows in the empty frame and makes the upstairs doors thud and rattle, as though someone is up there all the time. Ghosts of children playing, and a cripple who hobbles now and again about the bare wood floor.

Well, I have asked him. Noel is real. That much is quite true. He is over at this place near Salisbury, as Olive wrote. There is no reason to doubt that she went there to see him, and he was as she described.

But Edward's son. Hers. Edward and Olive. All that time ago. And *since*; what of that? How could it have been the way she said—and then nothing? Something must have lasted over. Either they would have got rid of the memory and never seen each other again, or it went on, with them seeing each other every day, thrown together constantly, and sharing the same interests, under the same roof.... But hiding it all so cleverly, so that even I, who thought I knew them, had no idea. Thought of themselves as brother and sister, so that sex between them became impossible? Or acknowledged incest?

She had made herself forget, not Noel but her own part in him. She remembered Edward's bastard son, but not that she had been his mother. How could anyone forget a thing like that—without they were mad? Without it became so loathsome that her mind denied the reality of it? That was the beginning of it all, when the fine hair-split first showed. Schizophrenia, isn't it? And then, after Martine died, in shock she made herself remember again, gathered her split mind together, like an athlete drawing himself in before some prodigious leap, and then—killed herself. No, the end's all wrong. She shouldn't have *died*. Somehow it went wrong. Fenella was going to die; *she* was to survive. And replace Fenella. She says so more than once. I must find the place. Yes, take over from Fenella. Go back to Greenshards. Become Giles Blanchard's wife.

But that means it was Giles, not Edward, she loved by then. Or, more likely, was it really Greenshards? It seems to have exercised a mystic hold over her. That was the first thing at the seance that came through her, that conversation with her father about the fragments of ancient glass he dug up in the garden. There were two voices; I heard them, Edward too. One a man, one a child. I've never known her mimic, but she might have done the child's. Did Giles produce the man's voice? But Edward recognised it, or was persuaded he did. Perhaps we were all over-suggestible that night and Olive herself mentions they may have used hallucinogenic drugs. Whatever the truth, behind it appears the same evil face. Giles Blanchard. He could have partly hypnotised us all.

But then Fenella said something more. About death. Cypresses, that was it—and at first it came through as 'Cyprus', but another voice corrected it. A poem by D. H. Lawrence about priests and choristers. A burial. And then she spoke of the 'white bird, all broken'— which mistakenly we took for the Fenwicks' plane. But Olive finally read it as a small, stone sparrow on the edge of our bird-bath. Did that suggest to her how the prediction might come true? Is that when she decided to kill her own niece? *Martine, my baby?* How she must have hated me! Because I had Edward, and his two healthy, normal children.

There was something else Fenella said at the end. 'Whatever will poor Giles do now?' Something like that. And Olive never remembered those words after Martine was dead. At first she had thought they referred to Fenella's death. How could they relate to Martine's? Unless she was acknowledging it all done under his influence, that evil, monstrous man. Was Fenella, in a genuine clairvoyant moment, asking herself what lengths he would next go to in ruining our lives?

It's no good. I get nowhere. The questions go round and round, never leading to answers but only to more like themselves.

And just such a turmoil as this Edward has been living with and suffering for days, weeks and more, since he first found the manuscript where Olive left it in his desk. Edward who, as she said, has such a conscience; is all conscience. How can he bear it? He must see himself as responsible for all that happened. Because, in the first place, of a pitiful romantic attachment he had as a boy for his crippled cousin. And ever since, all he has done, from sympathy and decency, has added to the injury, has made reality less and less acceptable for her until finally—

But what exactly *did* she do? And where does Giles Blanchard come in?

The answers are at Greenshards. Somehow I shall have to pull myself together and brave them. I don't know how to start, what to say. Perhaps I should try to tell Anne-Marie what has happened, so that she may recognise her husband as the monster he is. But she must already have become reconciled to that. She, if anyone, must have more proof than I could ever find.

If only Edward were capable of action. But he suffers so, and does nothing else! He lets it beat him. When I asked questions he made no attempt to explain or excuse himself. He is used to the idea of Noel, but he can't see that to me—I have to accept it, yes, but little by little, and not tied up in this complication of Olive's madness. He doesn't see this, he doesn't appear troubled about how I may take it. All that matters to him is Olive, what she thought of him, how suffering sent her insane.

Well, I am sorry for her too. But more than that—I am afraid. For the rest of us: Andrew, Edward and me. We're still alive, and so still vulnerable. Unless we do something to halt Giles Blanchard there is more he may do to us. Why am I the only one that can see this?

I tried to tell Sammy, but Giles was at him first. There is only one way to read that little walk Olive took him before his official meeting with the Blanchards. Giles had been warned by her before to stay away when Sammy came, but this second time he'd had the chance to make plans. Olive never explained her motives for taking Sammy to the boathouse, and she didn't have to. Giles was waiting for them there: Giles had commanded her to bring his next victim. So, in the half-dark, he was able to hypnotise him without Sammy's realising. Nothing I could have told him after that, and no evidence of his own eyes, would have made any difference. His mind had been made up: Giles Blanchard was above reproach, and both he and 'Fenella' were to be accepted without question as the couple Sammy had known all those years before.

I should have guessed this myself. On one count Olive was right: Sammy was a fool. And what does that make me, to be so taken up with that stupid affair when my family was under attack from a devil? God, it sounds mediaeval! Like witches and curses and that bloody Lady of Shalott. No wonder Edward, with his insistence on evidence—the truth, the whole truth and nothing but the limited, legalistic truth—just can't cope.

Edward, don't you see? It's not *impossible*. It's age-old human experience: black magic in the sixteenth century, psychiatry in the present. Not mere poetic fabrication, but real. What did she do, the Lady of Shalott? For some reason she never understood, she made herself live a strange, tormented life at one remove from the world. She believed herself bewitched, and so she was. She broke her own rules (it doesn't matter whether imposed by herself or another) and, believing she must die for it, she died. People are doing that all the time, all around us: believing something so that it becomes true. Minds are not the tiny, tidy things you imply in documents. If you understood that, you could begin to fight back. At least you could accept what Olive did to herself, and it would go easier with you.

The real issue isn't poor Olive, (and I do truly pity her, for all she libelled me most savagely and must have hated me in her warped and envious soul) no, it's not her dilemma but ours, now. What are we to do?

Olive's testament explains so much, but it proves nothing. It would be useless at the local police station. They would never get past the scandal. They'd relish the House of Usher details, and go on tipping their helmets to the Blanchards, sympathising that they'd got themselves involved with such a wildly mad and immoral family as us. The fact we've lived here, in normal guise, among them for so many years, would only blacken the case against us, accentuating the deceit. They would take it out on us that they'd once thought us worth looking up to. No, it's unthinkable. Olive's papers will have to be destroyed. I wish to God Giles had found them when he was searching, and taken them right away. What misery they've caused already. I never needed to know about Edward's childhood affair and the baby. It happened so long before we met. And although it's easy enough to deny everything she says about Sammy and me, how can Edward really continue to believe in me? My only hope is that under shock from learning about Olive he overlooked some details. He has never mentioned our affair, never levelled any accusations. If only he doesn't understand that Andrew has guessed about us.

I can't leave it until Andrew's home. He already knows too much. I shall have to go to Plymouth myself, immediately. Whatever proof Edward needs to convince him that Giles is behind all this wickedness, is down there, in some newspaper office. Any enquiry would come better from Edward, as a solicitor, but he would never find what he doesn't wish to be there. Even if I could persuade him to go, I couldn't trust him to search. But I shall find it. I am determined; perhaps that's why Giles has never been able to dominate me. I am not a dreamer like Olive, but active. And Olive never hated enough: I can, and I do.

It was a false-Spring day, with glancing sunlight; warm in the car, but when you stepped out, the wind was at you, cutting and whipping your legs. It made the sea crisp, with white edges, and the houses were white too, but cold to the touch. Clumps of stiff daffodils in the city's green patches had no golden joy, but shone a sour yellow.

I was fooled at first. By the clear air, the flowers, the pleasant girl in the newspaper office. I settled in comfortably with my load of back copies, and eventually I found the case I was looking for. The inquest, and a week before it, the account of the fire, with pictures.

The *au pair* girl's name was Elisabeth. Elisabeth Kruger, a fine-boned blonde. Her remains had been shipped back to her family in Cologne. There was no mention of any Anne-Marie. I began to be mortally afraid.

There was nothing for it but to get back in the car and drive home. I had nothing to show Edward. Thank God I hadn't told him where I was bound for that day.

Back with Olive's manuscript, and re-reading and re-reading it. Finding with every page some new horror I hadn't recognised at first. How many times had Edward done this, alone in his study, dipping into this nightmare that he'd feel responsible for creating?

But he wasn't the villain of the piece at all. I began to see a new one, like Olive once said—an indistinct shadow. And sometimes it looked like the outline of Giles Blanchard, and then sometimes like Olive herself. And sometimes, God help me, it was me.

No, that way lies more suffering and madness. I think we shall have to go through it together, Edward and I, soberly and humbly, and I shall have to admit to whatever of her accusations were true, to be able to clear

myself of her unjust libels. And he can do the same. I
can reassure him about so much. At least we shall be
together again, which we haven't been for so long. Perhaps we can share some of the guilt and so make it less.

He won't listen. He just sits there and lets me read
some part of it to him, and when I stop I see his mind is
far away. He even tries to be patient with me, as though
it is I who have to be humoured: and then when I try
to reason with him there's a look almost of distaste that
crosses his face, and he turns away again. I would be glad,
I think, if he even accused me directly. Of infidelity,
adultery, anything big enough to be able to say I'm
sorry for. It's the little things that Olive has poisoned
him with. Her insistence on my failures in the home, the
way she always managed to be there when I was missing,
the things she quotes that make me sound so *shallow*.
I'm not, Edward. I'll prove it to you. Only give me time.
And listen to me. You have to believe how vindictive she
had become at the last, and twisted. She libelled me
foully, eaten up with jealousy because I had you and the
children, while she had nothing, no one, had even lost
Greenshards which was all she'd ever really cared for in
her life.

Only, you don't want to believe me. Especially if it
means seeing her as anything less than perfect. She has
the insuperable advantage of being dead, while I can go
on making more mistakes.

Yes, I only harm myself in his eyes by finding any
fault in her. It is Giles Blanchard he must learn to blame,
and it's certainly true that he's been the evil genius all

through. If I can't prove he killed his first wife, at least I can underline how Olive believed he intended Fenella dead. If the saintly Olive thought that, and was in her turn used as his cat's-paw, surely Edward can produce enough anger on her behalf to arouse him from this awful, morbid apathy of guilt.

He seems to go a little way with me on this. But not far enough. He quoted Olive at me, that I was always wanting to apportion blame: that that was my normal reaction to grief. *He* didn't want to blame, but to understand.

I pleaded with him to consider, if not the past, the *future* dangers—to us, to Andrew, to the girl who called herself Anne-Marie.

I told him I knew now she wasn't the *au pair* girl supposed burnt to death ten years ago, but still she wasn't the real Fenella. She was some other girl Giles had picked up on the way. Edward must admit that much was true, because he'd heard himself how she answered my question after the crash. Before Giles had been able to get at her, she'd clearly said, 'I am Anne-M...'.

But Edward stood there shaking his head at me. 'No,' he said. 'Oh no. That wasn't what she said. You're mistaken, Megan. What she said was, 'I am *Anima*!'

5

HE BELIEVES OLIVE entirely! Literally. Because her poor split mind made her think that at times she could leave her body, because she had some success with telepathy, because she saw Fenella as a vacuum and herself entering it by what she called a psychical implosion —Olive really believed (or at least for a part of the time believed) that after death she could take over Fenella's body. Well, Olive believed it, yes. But not Edward, not the stable, logical, legalistic Edward. Is he so much a Minton too that he can't escape the taint?

As Olive insists so often in her testament, they are two of a kind. But that doesn't mean they must see all things the same way, in the same supernatural light. But suffering unhinged her, as now it seems to have done him.

There is the big difference, though, that Olive is dead and Edward lives on. I can help him.

I could help him, if he would let me. If he sees himself at all, which I doubt, it must surely be as between Olive and me. And she is endowed with supernatural powers, while I'm only human, and an empty shell. I've failed him so often already, while she has always been in the right, wronged.

I actually pitied her, when all the time the web she wove had such powerful magic that it destroyed not only her but anyone who becomes aware of it now that she's gone.

That is the true nature of the Lady of Shalott's curse: her lifetime's working of fantasy into the fabric of a frustrated mind, so that its woof and warp become the very ganglia of living evil. All her lifetime, all her powers, went to perfect her own destruction.

Olive Minton, you're dead! Over, done with. All that ever contained your life is out there in Garroway's Field, under the new grave. That is why we bury with such ceremony, isn't it?—pressing you dead back with each firmed-in polyanthus, weighing you under with granite chips and marble kerb. So that you may stay so.

Leave us to our living. *We* are in charge. *We* have to make the decisions, not go on suffering yours.

Perhaps it has done some good after all, to speak directly to Edward. Since that incredible claim he made that Fenella thought herself Anima, he has been more calm and relaxed. He has lost the somnambulist look and appears more like a convalescent. He must see now, once it has been put into words, how far from reality his mind was leading him. He has been twice into the office this week and I understand from Jo Carpenter that the accountants have been called in, on Edward's suggestion. That can only mean that he is taking an interest again in the practice and making an attempt to get things back under his own control. At times I find him too with his eyes on me, as though considering what I said. It is hard then not to go on and say more, but I have this intuition that it would be wrong. He must work it out for himself. I see now what I never knew before, that explaining and understanding are a very long way apart; not complementary, but even perhaps exclusive of each other.

He goes quite often into Greenshards' garden of an evening, and I think he stands there in the shadow of our hedge, looking over at the house, working things out. I haven't dared to follow him. Again I have this feeling that it would be fatal to interfere. But I wish he would reach a conclusion soon. I have never been good at waiting.

We have received a small engraved card from the Blanchards, announcing they will be 'At Home' on Thursday evening before leaving for a holiday in America. Below the formal invitation to drinks someone had written, by hand, 'We do hope you will both stay on afterwards for dinner.' Then the initials F. and G. It is the first time I have seen the writing of either of them. For that matter, it is the first time they have invited us other than by word of mouth.

Edward has said he would like to accept. In fact, he assumed immediately that we should be going. I should have thought he'd prefer to stay away from them when they've caused our family such grief. However, if he is seriously considering Giles' guilt, perhaps it is as well that he should get a chance to study him at nearhand and possibly catch him out with a few careful questions. This will be the first time I have spoken to them for nearly a fortnight, although I have watched Fenella walking in the garden and poking about among the bulbs. She gets stronger daily and walks almost normally now.

There was such a crowd there. I hadn't realised the Blanchards knew so many local people. And there were some too who weren't from hereabouts. The Fenwicks were again numbered among the guests, as Fenella had handed over the catering to a hotel. It reminded me of that other night when Mrs. Fenwick had first removed her apron and joined in with the seance. She was certainly something more than an ordinary housekeeper. I determined, after the second drink, that since Fenella and Giles were taken up with their social duties, I couldn't do better than corner the Fenwicks, separately if possible, and find out as much as I could of their past.

It wasn't hard to get started, for the woman came up with her smooth, cool smile to where I found myself in a group discussing holidays. Bevis was one of them, with his new tennis coach he seemed bent on advertising; and Mortimer, the manager where Giles banks; and Maud Cudlip who writes romance for teenagers. Maud goes across to the U.S. for about six weeks every year on a business and lecturing tour.

"Have you ever been to the States, Mrs. Fenwick?" she asked, taking the initiative away from me.

The housekeeper smiled and revolved her glass between long fingers. "Oh yes, certainly I have." She looked at me mockingly, I thought. "As a matter of fact it was there..."

Giles came bouncing into our group. "I do want you to meet ... know you're always so pleased to have new

164

neighbours." He went on about some little, round woman who had taken one of the converted cottages past old Mr. Blackstock's, and Mrs. Fenwick turned away, her words spilling into the bedlam of conversation. I had to shout as I followed her, "You were saying...?" But she shook her head, made a hopeless little gesture with her hands to show she couldn't compete with the general noise and managed to slide away from me. Old Dr. Hepworth clawed at me from a ring of hospital personalities and I had to endure another heated discussion about the rival claims of airbeds and extra physiotherapy equipment on the endowment fund. When I struggled free of that group I tried to find Edward. As soon as I began asking for him, I saw Fenwick look up across the room and start moving through the crowd towards us. I let him catch up and made some laughing remark about packing luggage to suit air travel limits. He appeared very relaxed and said the Blanchards would be travelling light anyway. The heavy stuff would go on by sea later.

"So it will be a long stay?" I asked. "Things will be very quiet for you here when they've gone."

"I understand the house will be closed all summer," he said. "We'll be away ourselves in a week or two."

"To the States as well?"

He laughed. "I shouldn't imagine so. It depends who advertises the sort of job we're looking for."

"You mean you're leaving here for good?"

"That's right," he said easily. "It would be rather a waste of our time looking after an empty house, wouldn't it?"

So there was no intimate Blanchard-Fenwick connection after all. My intuition that they'd been together before the move to Greenshards seemed mistaken. "I thought," I said hesitantly, "you'd been with the Blanchards for a long time."

"About four years," he said. "They've been lovely people to work for, but one likes a change, however sad one is to lose them."

"Have you ever been to America?" I asked, since I'd nothing else then to say.

"Oh yes," said Fenwick. "That's where we met up. We were all on the same bill, so to speak."

What on earth he meant by that I was never to learn, because just at that moment the caterer came up with some query and Fenwick asked me to excuse him. I put my question and its curious answer into a niche in my mind, meaning to bring the subject up later when the main guests had gone, and then I ran into Jo Carpenter who was looking for Fenella to say goodbye.

We moved out into the hall and I was relieved to see the crowd thinning. I had the idea that because Fenella and Edward were nowhere to be seen they must be together, but just then she came out of the study with Watson, who is senior partner in the rival chambers to Edward's. It struck me as rather funny for the moment to see him where I'd expected my husband. Edward, I discovered a few minutes later, was sitting slouched on a teak bench on the terrace, fast asleep. I suppose that shouldn't have surprised me, for he sleeps little at night and sometimes walks for what seems hours about the house in the dark. Yet seeing him there like that I was afraid. I thought back to when I'd last seen Giles near him and knew I should never have risked leaving Edward alone when he was about.

He awoke normally when I touched him, glanced shamefacedly about and apologised. He seemed all right; he had always hated the neck-stretching, squawking crowds you get at this sort of party. We went indoors together and I found him a whisky standing ready poured on a tray of filled glasses. Remembering how Olive had been afraid of drugs, I was afraid for him too, being so like her and liable to be influenced in the same way. Only it wouldn't be Giles getting at him, of course, but Fenella. Was there an affinity? I asked myself. Where had this idea come from that Fenella might try making him conscious of her sexually?

The last guests were beginning to remind each other of later engagements. There were little scurries about for mislaid handbags, cars reversing over the gravel, windows wound down for hand waves and shouted greetings. Everyone seemed buoyant and louder than life. The Blanchards would be well remembered when they were gone.

I stood in the hall with Edward and the house changed about us, growing colder. Even though the lights were left full on, you could feel the shadows come closer.

Fenella shuddered wryly at the litter of glass and used china, the choked ashtrays and general disorder. "Let's forget it," she said, and led us through to the glazed sun lounge where a small dinner table was set for four. From the opposite door the little dachshund burst in and flung itself upon her. She whipped it up and crooned at the

queer little creature, pirouetting with it in her arms like
Olive used to with the babies. She seemed completely to
have forgotten she was recuperating from a serious illness. Giles came over fast and took the dog from her.
"Darling," he said, "I do believe you're tiddly."

"Origami ears," Fenella said, pulling at the silky fur.
"No, I haven't had very much to drink. Tonight I could
have been as happy on distilled water. Truly. And yet
it's a sad occasion. I don't think now I want to go away.
Must we, Giles? Can't we just huddle inside the house
when it's shut up, and pretend we've gone?"

I looked then at Edward, and he was smiling at her.
Fondly. And she gazed back. They appeared unaware of
anyone else in the world. It was naïve; so young. I turned
sickly away and almost ran into Giles' stare. He had
seen it too, and was furious.

I knew then, in an intuitive flash, how greatly things
had altered at Greenshards. It was as though Giles and
Fenella had changed places. He had always looked much
older, but now he was—*senescent*, I suppose. Failing, in
a way; while Fenella, older too than when she'd come
here nearly a year ago, was developed. She had acquired
a sort of ageless maturity. All the time since her accident
she had been growing more positive. She was the one
now who initiated things, made suggestions, planned,
and Giles watched in baffled disbelief. Somewhere she
had found the power to master him, and the energy to
use that power. I wondered suddenly if she had begun to
blackmail him.

"I thought," I said, "it was your idea to take this
holiday?"

168

It took some seconds for everyone to adjust to the question, so preoccupied were they all with their own private thoughts. Then Fenella shrugged. She made a little balancing movement with one hand. "Yes and no," she said. "I was told a change would do me good, and an English Spring can be very long a-coming. I agreed to go."

"Perhaps it will do Giles good too," I suggested with a touch of malice.

The other two looked then at Giles as though he had just become visible. He stared back at me with something like resentment.

"It will," said Fenella more gently. "He has had a great deal to put up with lately."

"I hope," I told them, "he'll have a chance to relax, when you're away from here."

They all knew what I meant. That was the mockery of the rest of the evening—the fact that we all understood, and refused to speak outright. We made a play at being neighbourly, while under the veneer of sophistication we were aware of the primitive lusts and hates that moved us.

I thought the time for us to leave would never come. When at last I stood in the hall with my coat over my shoulders, Edward still turned back. He felt wretched; I felt it too, for him. "You will come back?" he asked soberly. "There isn't any chance that...?" His head moved so that although he held Fenella's hands, it was Giles he questioned.

Giles said nothing, just smiled, for the first time since the other guests had left.

"I shall be back," Fenella said quietly. "You can be sure of that. I love Greenshards, and what should I do without the Mintons?"

She meant it. And strongly as I hated her then, I must admit she seemed to include me. It wasn't just Edward.

"Remember me," she said softly, "to Andrew when he gets home on Saturday. I'm so sorry to have missed him." Again she sounded utterly sincere, although Andrew and she never have had time for each other.

"Goodbye," I said, hugging my coat about me so that I shouldn't have to endure touching either of them. Then, abruptly, I went off and Edward was obliged to come after.

They left next day immediately after lunch, and the Fenwicks lowered the blinds on the south side of the house. It looked as though someone was dead.

6

LIFE WITH THEM gone has been more endurable. A
week has passed without so much as a postcard to remind
us they exist. Andrew has managed to distract Edward,
and they have even planned one or two trips together,
but most days Edward has gone in to the office for four
or five hours. I wish I could really believe that everything is all right now.

On Easter Monday two men came to the house. It
used not to be unusual for Edward to ask clients up here
when they had urgent business over public holidays, but
these men were different. I was a little curious but didn't
go out of my way to ask him who they were. It was
Andrew who came, bubbling with scandal, to tell me.

"What does Dad want detectives for?" he demanded.

"You mean, what do they want him for?" I corrected.

"No," he said impatiently, "it's not that way round.
He's employing them. There was a letter from their
agency out on his desk before they came. It was signed
by someone called Hubard. And that's what I heard him
call one of them. Hubard and Hopkins, Private Investigators. It sounds like a TV series."

Edward doesn't touch divorces. Unless, perhaps, his
own?

"Are you admitting to reading other people's corres-
pondence?" I asked Andrew, almost mechanically.

He'd just happened to see it, he said. Well, it couldn't have been anything particularly private or it wouldn't have been left out in the open, would it?

Not unless that was Edward's tactfully oblique way of bringing the matter to my mind. But what reason would he have suddenly to want more information about Sammy and me, when he must for some time have had all he needed for a separation? No, I don't think it's that.

I asked him after supper tonight what case he'd put those investigators on. He raised his eyebrows as though my ignorance surprised him.

"They're looking into the Blanchards," he said simply. "Isn't that what you've always wanted?"

Well, I did. When they were still here. But now the best thing is to forget them. And anyway it's Giles we need investigated; emphasise that, *Giles*. To look into Fenella might be stirring up unwanted trouble.

I made some noncommittal answer and went to clear the dishes. When I came back with coffee I found him in the hall, leaning weakly against the front door. It was unlocked behind him and he seemed to have just come in.

"What is it?" I called out.

His face was papery and he kept his eyes down, moved his lips as though speaking, but no sound came. I led him to the settle and he sat there, back against the wall, then leant and put his face in both hands.

"The dog," he said, when he could speak again.

"What—?"

"Olive's," he said. "I went across to see Fenwick. I thought—rather than have the thing go into kennels

172

when they shut up the house—I'd offer to have it here. But it's gone. She took it with her."

"You mean, Fenella took it? To America?"

"Yes. You see what it means? She'd never leave it there. And return quarantine's out of the question. She wouldn't put it through all that."

So, she isn't coming back! Despite what she said at the last, we shan't be seeing Fenella again. Oh, I'm glad, glad, *glad*.

I thought it was all over, but I was too eager to believe what I wanted to hear. Even then there were moments when I asked myself why Fenella should let a dog make so much difference. Then I'd go out, through the beech hedge, and look at the closed house. I'd remember that the Fenwicks were paid off and had taken a position on some big estate near Peterborough. I would tell myself it was all finished, there was no likelihood of Giles allowing Fenella to come back here where she might see Edward again. She would have to play him up pretty badly away, before he preferred to run that risk. And then Edward himself was so sure that they didn't intend coming back.

It was sometime in June that I heard the house was up for sale. Watson mentioned it to Carpenter and Jo leaked it to me. She was obviously intrigued that Giles had picked on the rival firm when we were such close neighbours and had handled other business for them. She hinted at some little quarrel between our two families, but I was able to turn it aside.

"How tactful of him," I said. "He must have known

how fond of Greenshards Edward's always been, and having to sell it again would bring back so many sad memories. Now isn't that just like Giles, to be so thoughtful?" And the hypocrisy didn't stick in my throat at all, for I was so happy to be proved right. I could afford a compliment for the Blanchards, when I felt so safe and distant from them.

All through the summer people came and looked over the house, but the SOLD notice never went up. "Nor ever is likely to, while they're asking such a sum," Jo Carpenter commented.

She seemed to delight in acting as go-between, carrying news from one office to the other. She was developing into a regular tittle-tattle, and I caught her more than once probing into Edward's intentions with regard to the partnership. I was glad to be able to say that I'd no idea what his professional plans were. He was attending the office more regularly than he had done for some time, and although his work was of little interest to me this seemed to be a healthy sign, so I encouraged it. Apart from his work, however, he took no pleasure in anything, and we were as far apart as at any point since Olive's death.

"Who set the price so high?" I asked idly.

"Oh, she did," Jo replied. "Against advice, but what can you do? Greenshards is in her name after all."

It had an ominous ring to it. Fenella's name was recurring far too often for someone we were none of us going to see again.

And then, one autumn afternoon, I looked across and the blinds were raised at all the south windows. I phoned Jo Carpenter on some slight pretext and she told me there was a caretaker in residence. Giles Blanchard had been anxious about the state and safety of the furniture, so he'd wanted everything put in store. He'd authorised a depository to take delivery, but before they'd been able to make the arrangements, Fenella had written to cancel the order. Giles, apparently, had suddenly been taken ill and was in hospital recovering from a coronary. Until he was able to send fresh directions, all was to stay as it was, but with a caretaker to keep an eye on security.

"Does that mean," I asked heavily, "they'll be coming back as soon as Giles is well enough to travel?"

Jo shrugged. "Read it however you like," she said, "but there's one significant factor: she's put up the price even higher."

I wondered how much Edward knew about what was going on, and whether he'd even had some direct communication from them that I didn't know of. There was evidently some covert struggle going on between the Blanchards themselves, a power contest of which I'd glimpsed the iceberg-tip that last evening we dined with them at Greenshards. And at the present Fenella had the upper hand.

Today Edward arrived home unexpectedly from the office at lunchtime. It didn't matter, for there was enough in the fridge for a twosome emergency. But he wasn't hungry. He went through to the study, saying he'd make do with coffee. As a sort of after-thought he said, "Bring in a cup for yourself too. I want to talk to you."

He was looking tired, but not ill. More serious than

anything. But not tragic. I didn't feel frightened, or think Andrew had met with some accident: it wasn't like that. But just as I poured boiling water in the stone coffee pot we use when there are only the two of us, I stopped. Into my mind came the words, 'For the last time'. And then more than words, a complete desolation, as though I had reached the end of existence.

It was uncanny, and quite unrelated to any recognisable cause. But I experienced it, without understanding. I suppose that is how Olive felt that morning in the linen-room when Martine burst in with the news that the Blanchards had come. Only her intuition was of a beginning. Mine is of an end. Opposites which are the same to some extent. Both deeply disturbing.

When I felt able to face Edward, I took in the tray. He was very gentle and cleared a space for me to put it on the desk in front of him. As though I were an invalid, I let him pour the coffee.

"You didn't see *The Times* this morning?" he asked.

I never do. We have the *Telegraph* delivered here, and his *Times* goes to the office direct. He brings it home and I usually glance at it in the evenings. He repeated his question and I shook my head.

He took it, ready folded, and put it down in front of me. He pointed to the obituary column.

Giles Farnworth Blanchard, aged fifty-two, after a short illness, in a nursing home at Acapulco, October 31st.

Giles Blanchard dead. I couldn't for a moment speak. When I did, I said, "Hallowe'en." Such a stupid thing to say.

"What does it mean?" I asked next. "What has this to do with me?"

He didn't answer immediately. He looked down at his hands, opened them and looked long at their backs as though they were something new worthy of being learned. Then, "Drink up," he said kindly, "or your coffee will be cold."

I flung it at him. Some went over his face and stung his cheek a fiery red, and some went past on to the ivory wallpaper and left a mark like some huge, obscene, brown spider whose legs started dropping longer and longer, stiltlike, till they reached the wainscot and then must have gone on, lengthening under the carpet, out of the room, over the garden, reaching out for ever—but by then the spider had become a grotesque, spiked balloon sailing on innumerable cords and it dangled there, out of reach of some child that had watched it rise. And the child howled and screamed in fury while it sailed away, out of reach for ever.

I saw all this and heard it, while Edward sat, unmoving, and coffee dripped from the angle of his jaw to the white of his shirt and the grey of his office suit. And his face I shall never forget. It was as though he endured what he must and what he had known had to be, but that once it was done it was done for all time and he would be glad it was finished. Suffering so, and ashamed for me, and so damned Minton *right*!

He doesn't have to tell me. I should never have asked. What Giles Blanchard's death has to do with me is this; that Fenella is free now and she wants my husband.

I behaved like a fishwife, but what else can I do? I have

never suffered in silence like the noble Mintons. What right had he to marry me? He belongs to his own kind, with all this Minton sensitivity and fineness. It's not fair that they should set themselves up alongside me and make me out so crude. I was alive, happy, successful in my way. And five senses were enough to live by. But they must have more. Well, I am human, no more. And by God it hurts!

7

MY DEAR MEGAN,

When this reaches you, you will already know that I have left. I think you know where I have gone and what I shall be looking for. It must be obvious too that I have been prepared for this for some time. I have not planned that it should come about quite in this way, I have merely known it would be so. Perhaps when you have had time to think, and remember, you will see that you too had certain premonitions.

What I shall find at the end of my journey I do not know. I am trying to travel with an open mind. But you must understand—I believe you do—that there is much I have to make amends for. I am very conscious of my shortcomings, towards you as well as to others whose debt I have been in for much longer. Now I intend to do whatever seems right (or the lesser evil) with all of you in mind.

Please believe that I still admire you enormously. It would be impossible to try and assess how great a blessing you have been to me. Your vitality made me alive in my turn. Your energy and cheerfulness were an inspiration. You were more than I deserved. You were all that, at one time, I would have liked myself to be. And the children have much of you in them. But none of you has need of me any more.

I have done what I can over the past few months to ensure that you will never be in financial need. My withdrawal from the firm has been carefully organised and requires only a signature to make it complete. I have invested carefully on your behalf, and although one can never cover all eventualities, there is a good basis to work on, and the firm will always advise and guide you as trustees. I should like the house to be sold and have already ordered this put in motion. You have never been a countrywoman at heart, and I am sure you will not stay long away from London once you feel yourself free. I wish you every happiness there, or wherever you find it more attractive to go. Perhaps you will marry again; I hope so, for essentially you like to belong. If you will accept Sammy, I think you will give him the stability he needs. I have no fears for you, because you are the kitten who always falls on her feet. You will be angry with me, and rightly, but soon you will be smiling again.

I am leaving to you Olive's testament, for I know it almost by heart and you will want to read it over from time to time. There is so much in it one has to learn to understand. It is a record of suffering and enlightenment and love. Yet only once in it did she use that last word—of her childhood love affair. But she was all love in her service to us, and that is what we denied her in return. Or, in my case, tried to stifle. Whatever she did, or perhaps tried unsuccessfully to do, was a labour of faithfulness. The least I can do is go after her and find if she achieved the impossible. In any case, wherever she has gone I shall follow, because I love her and she still needs me. It seems a hopeless hope, but I believe in what she wrote. And in her case, she said it was only Merlin she glimpsed on the road to Camelot; Lancelot was another. She is waiting for me and I must go at once.

Blame me if you will, but, Megan, also understand,

With my love,

Edward.

8

I HAVE MADE a selection of what Edward would have called 'the documents in the case'. Firstly there is Olive's testament, which either started everything off or is itself an account of whatever was the beginning. Then come my letters returned so hurtfully by Sammy. I have read them through again and really they are relevant because they carry on the thread and show besides how ignorant I was of what was happening at the time. I have included as well two I wrote to Andrew which came home in the trunk. And Edward's letter, which should have made everything clear but is itself as open to varying inter- pretations as was the worst of Olive's metaphysical tangle.

And then there is this that I am writing now. It doesn't begin 'Dear—' because there is no one left to write to: I know now there never was. Sammy didn't matter, didn't ever exist for me as a person. He was an excuse I gave myself. He was on the receiving end of my casting and direction, not positive enough to have a part specially written in, but conveniently negative, so that I could make of him what I needed. And I needed a confidant, a pseudo-lover, a blank wall to practise my shadows against. Now even that delusion is finished, and I fall back on writing to myself—Olive's device.

Over these past few days, alone in this silent house, it has sometimes seemed to me that I am growing like her;

as if she is some malignant form of life feeding on us until we are all totally absorbed, and so become a part of her.

Could it conceivably be that she did have strange powers, and really could, while she lived, float in and out of others' minds? Things did happen at the seances when she was willing to fix her concentration on our chosen object. I saw that myself, I acknowledge it. And other strange things she mentioned in her account were at least half true. She must have warned Giles and Fenella away that first weekend I invited Sammy down here. But how? She certainly never left the room while Edward and I were arguing about my plan to unmask them. So she must have managed to send a message later, which I don't see was possible, or else went to him disembodied, while we both saw her sitting there in the same room with us, not moving. And that earlier occasion when she claims to have done the same—or does she?—no, she wrote that she had stolen out to Greenshards while Martine was absorbed in her game of Halma, and crept back unobserved, all between our leaving Giles and arriving back by the two long driveways. At that time, when she wrote, she really believed she had gone there in the flesh. But she was wearing her housecoat; Olive would never have called on anyone dressed like that. It was not all imagined, dreamt up in a nodding moment, for she described so perfectly Fenella's dress and the hall, which was a room I never mentioned to her when I got back, because to my mind it was so plain the way they'd had it done. And the way she wrote, the tenses she used, imply that she sat down almost immediately afterwards to set out her account. If only Martine were still able to tell us what happened that night, whether she did notice her aunt leave the room at all. And another strange thing happened about then, for that was when Edward heard Martine playing the Chopin Ballade, which would have been physically impossible even on a warm night with all the windows opened, which it wasn't.

No, I have to accept that at times the unaccountable has happened. To some extent. Researches into extra-sensory perception confirm other cases in the experience of reliable, rational people. There are masses of books in the library that witness to it, and they are written by men and women of intelligence and integrity. I had previously thought that the Society for Psychical Research was a set of gullible cranks, but it appears not. Its members are highly respected, detached observers, scientists in their own right. They concede the possibility of perception beyond the commonly accepted physical limits. It's terrifying to think that while we go on with our everyday preoccupations, there is this other world there, parallel to our own, almost open to exploration if we only knew how, a whole new dimension of living that may become available to future human beings. Some day humanity will look back from over that threshold and see *us* as limited and deprived, just as we regard mankind before speech, or without fire.

And yet something in me refuses to accept the pos-sibility, something built-in, that acknowledges only the limitation of the senses. Perhaps, as Olive experienced, there are the two lives inside oneself, one centred on the brain and the other on something apart that uses it but is independent of it for existence. If so, then telepathy, clairvoyance and communication with the dead would be possible. And transmigration of this essence? Given a positive such as Olive, and a negative as in Fenella's case, could they have made such an exchange, on the very threshold of death?

It is easier, most of the time, to accept this mystery on the physical level of premeditated crime, to believe that we have all been made dupes of by a mad Svengali who wished to be rid of a wealthy but boring wife. He wasn't a psychiatrist as I'd at first thought, but an endocrinologist, so at least he had a good knowledge of the effects of drugs. It was Edward's investigators who unearthed that much when they traced Giles' medical career in the United States.

He had been quite brilliant in his own sphere and was researching at Columbia when he met Fenella Crosville, a young English starlet taking part in ESP experiments. The tests she was being put through were academic and deadly routine. She must have been bored to distraction, especially as her first outstanding successes had dwindled away until her number of 'hits' on standard tests now marked a curve well below the level of chance possibility. In this state of boredom and dejection, she was persuaded to go with him to Las Vegas and sit in at roulette. Immediately she began to win, and made such a killing there that the pair were warned off the circuit. (But they were back again as recently as four years ago—on which trip they attended a convention to do with ESP and there came into contact with the Fenwicks whose partner-

ship had fewer academic sources, being mainly in connection with entertainment and had more than a hint of
conmanship.)

After their first successes at the tables Giles and the
girl came over to England where he put in a great deal
of family-visiting with Fenella, and they finally received
permission for her to marry under age. Shortly before she
became Mrs. Blanchard she was left a considerable
fortune as main beneficiary in the will of an elderly
woman friend. The will, which completely reversed a
former one, was dated one month later than their return
from the United States. How sensitive I wonder, had the
old lady been to the combined powers of this charming
pair? Yet the money had been left conditionally, so that
Fenella enjoyed a set income for life, after which the
estate was to revert to a trust for the old lady's pet
charity. Which, eventually, may have suggested to Giles
the need for an immediate replacement whenever his
wife seemed on the point of extinction! Did he actually
achieve some such substitution after the fire which
wrecked their home and cost the life of a girl thought to
be the *au pair*? And, later, did he again attempt such a
coup, on a psychic level, to replace his second wife by
Olive, who had become, incredibly enough, his mistress?
Had the cool, knowledgeable criminal himself by then
become persuaded of the truth of his own psychic
fantasy?

I want to believe that: it leaves me off balance, true,
but still with my feet on the ground. I want to see the
whole macabre series of events as masterminded, deliberate and physical. All right then, Olive—I do want some-

one to blame. And it must, for sanity's sake, be Giles. Only, where is he now? Not supremely successful and more superbly confident than ever, but simply dead of a coronary thrombosis, and we all saw him failing and shrinking to his end. Not dead as Olive is, but utterly gone, without power of haunting. So was he the villain?

However that may be, it has come about that in our hearts not one of us believes the present 'Fenella' to be anyone other than Olive. There's no escaping it. Edward, who knew her so intimately and so long, thinks so; Giles was smugly sure of it; even the little dog that worshipped Olive was mad with delight at finding her again at Greenshards. And, more than anyone, the woman who goes by the name of Fenella Blanchard is convinced herself. Even while she was still in shock from the car crash, barely able to get the words out, she answered when I asked who she was—'I am *Anima*!'

Edward had the document at that time, and I had never so much as seen it. Giles hadn't either, so certainly the true Fenella couldn't have had access. But she used the secret name by which Olive called herself. She believes she is Olive. Shouldn't I go that little bit further and say she is? How else could she have known?

It is monstrous, hideous. I fear her as something ancient and terrible, a sort of Stonehenge that has been secretly alive and breathing for a thousand years. She would once have been burnt for a witch, *should have been*. We have to burn them to be safe ourselves.

Olive Minton, you are dead. *Dead!* Stay dead and leave the living alone.

Edward, can't you see? I am afraid for you. Mortally.

She still has power. Alive or dead. In Fenella, or else-where; even if totally extinguished as a person, some-thing goes on working itself out. In you.

It was always you. She possessed you once and is deter-mined to consume you again. Even if it means breaking down your sanity, making you run hopelessly after the shell of a stupid woman to recognise in her someone dead you fancy you once injured. She knows too well your conscience, how it hounds you. Oh, won't you *see*?

You do. While you deny it with one half of your mind —the outer, dried-up, legalistic shell—the crack appears. It sloughs off, a split husk. Something else emerges that belongs to her. And goes off, searching.

You write of 'going on a journey', 'travelling with an open mind', 'choosing the lesser evil' and 'wherever she has gone I shall follow'. To anyone outside this thing, reading it for the first time, the meaning would surely be clear. They would see your letter as a suicide note. You have tidied the future, as you see it, for Andrew and me, you have thanked us soberly for our worthy efforts, and chairmanlike gone out of office. Olive is dead and it is in death you go to find her.

But what am *I* to think—for I know the whole story, each of the possibilities. To me, it would seem that you have gone to find Olive alive. And if you find her, you may as well be dead, at least for me.

Ironically, you relinquish me to Sammy, a lover who has done with me already, whom I find now I never really wanted. Edward, there was only one man I ever truly loved, and that was you.

And suppose some day you come back. I don't know,

but you might. I shall have to wait a long while to find out. Not that we could ever be anything to each other again, except as reminders of failure.

That would be terrible, but at least something. What I fear more is this awful *nothing* stretching ahead. At night I dare not turn on the light till I have covered the windows, because I know now what she saw. I know it myself, the same terror at there being nothing beyond the black glass. In it only the reflection of myself; and a small, narrow room.

What is left to me now? This uncertain state we call sanity, and the slow passage to old age. The horror of going on and on and then finally ceasing. Surviving a while as a shadow projected on Andrew who follows. My son, who is your son too. A Minton. To end, perhaps, as mad as his father, and Olive, and *her* suicidal father, and his own bastard half-brother in the institution near Salisbury.

How has it all come about? Little more than eighteen months since those accursed people came to Greenshards. Better if it had been razed to the ground. New faces. 'Strange', Martine called them. *Diabolical*. My little girl, my baby.

I must get away from here, go up to London, lose myself among real, breathing people. Only, I'm not sure that I can stand the living yet. I am at some distance from them. It makes them alien; them or me.

Would it be like this if the Blanchards had never come? *Can* it all be Giles' fault, or have we helped each other to destroy him too?

Where did it all begin? When did we lose our innocence?

We have all lived in a protective glass house, but Olive found its tiny flaw. There was a minute, cratered hole through which a strange wind blew. Something abnormal found its way in to us.

Whether she was witch, or enchanted one, a pitiable psychopath, or the dupe of a modern Merlin, it was she who absorbed and distilled the evil for us others, all the time falsely decorous like a cameo whose model has carefully chosen her sweeter profile. She had us finely tied down with the thread of sewn-on buttons—and Sylko wound among crocuses—forever performing the trivial functions that made her necessary, while we did what we thought important. And all the time she was asserting her invisible power, tidying us away as she would our dirty shoes. Consuming (if we can believe her) first one man, and then another, with her unspeakable appetites, in (real or imagined) debauchery she describes as 'rites'. And all behind a homely, maiden front. One of those blessed meek who has found her own monstrous way of inheriting the earth!

Olive forever going on, that is the most terrifying possibility: the daemon running through all things, encountering no barrier between one being and the next, but absorbing, possessing, irrevocably growing like some voracious organism so that nothing is strong enough, far enough distant, to resist penetration. So that in the end we all become, to a greater or a less degree, Olive; and Olive, us transformed.

But I am not Olive. Her fantasies are not mine. Behind the drawn curtains here, I know, is the night of the garden; between it and me a pane of glass. It is whole and entire, unlike Olive's.

No, I am not Olive. I am different. Like the glass, I am whole. I am whole! *I am!*